Beautifully written and the subject ma [...] something wonderful here.

—James Van Praagh, best-selling author, internationally acclaimed spiritual teacher, and founder of the James Van Praagh School of Mystical Arts

A beautiful deeply moving and timeless story of relationships and love. It captures the readers' imagination, and you can become lost in your own story while reading it. It is hard to put down. You just want to know what happens next.

—Suellen Campbell, spiritual healer and teacher, Best of Health Australia Pty Ltd

Becoming Soul...an intriguing book that reminds us of the simplicity of life.... Readers of inspirational fiction, new age fiction, or religious spirituality will find this an inspiring and thought-provoking novel.

—Literary Titan

Becoming Soul leads by example... joining the human and the sacred in a warm, inviting text, ideal for Christian readers open to fresh spiritual ideas. A welcoming account of a reincarnated soul's sacred journey.

—BookLife Reviews

The book is best understood as an allegory for Jesus's own spiritual transformation...... Its own characters are developed in service of this....

—Foreword Reviews

..... relatable to those of any, or no, religion.......colorful, filled with incident, and touching....

—BlueInk Review

...... stirring to many, especially those with interest in New Age expressions of Christian faith...... significantly extends beyond a simple parable......unique and tough spiritual guide steeped in feminine love and divine compassion.

—Kirkus Review

Excellent at introducing New Age spiritual ideas...concepts are presented but never taught pedantically....author merits recognition as a writer but also as a spiritual teacher.

—The US Review of Books

Becoming Soul

Seven Steps to Heaven

El Alma

BALBOA.PRESS
A DIVISION OF HAY HOUSE

Balboa Press books may be ordered through booksellers or by contacting:

Balboa Press
A Division of Hay House
1663 Liberty Drive
Bloomington, IN 47403
www.balboapress.com.au
AU TFN: 1 800 844 925 (Toll Free inside Australia)
AU Local: (02) 8310 7086 (+61 2 8310 7086 from outside Australia)

Print information available on the last page.

ISBN: 978-1-5043-2086-3 (sc)
ISBN: 978-1-5043-2088-7 (hc)
ISBN: 978-1-5043-2087-0 (e)

Library of Congress Control Number: 2020903589

Balboa Press rev. date: 01/31/2023

There with the grace of God go I.

CONTENTS

INTRODUCTION

This story starts with the premise that we aren't our bodies. We start our journeys long before we arrive on earth, for we are our eternal consciousnesses. Our consciousnesses live on when we leave earth through death. It's only our bodies that decay and die. We are our souls. We continue to develop our souls during each lifetime we visit earth and then go back to being only consciousness.

In choosing a new lifetime on earth, there lies a quest in each of us to find our own souls' purposes for this lifetime and to find our way home by becoming souls again. Each soul knows that there are natural earth stages we each must endure to learn new lessons for our soul, and becoming soul again is the challenge of each lifetime. The stages can be broken down into seven steps that we need to pass through to arrive back to this eternal sacredness of our souls.

In reaching this inner realm, we'll be free to continue living on earth and become teachers to others on their souls' journeys to their inner sacredness. Or on the arrival at our inner realm, we can choose to leave earth and return to heaven. From there, we can choose to develop another lifetime and come back to earth to further our soul's lessons and become soul again.

The following seven steps to heaven will be included in each lifetime plan chosen by each of us:

Silence

Hope

Suffering

Loss

Survival

Believe

Heaven

These seven steps can be visualised as the steps Jesus chose to represent His story of love through His teachings, through His life and death on earth and through His resurrection to heaven. Jesus began His earthly life in danger. On the night He is born, authorities are already looking for Him and killing all boys under the age of two to make sure that He is killed with them. Angels from the spirit world tell His father to live and *survive* as refugees until they tell him it's safe to return to their home. Jesus *survives* a child's life undercover in *silence* and *hope* with His spiritually obedient parents.

When He is older, His parents fear they have lost Him. They are frantic when He wanders off on His own at a public gathering. They find Him conversing with and teaching the elders in the temple. His parents question Him, and He tells them that He is beginning His Soul's purpose by delivering His Father's message and breaking His *silence*. He also chooses to break His *silence* to change water into wine to publicise His soul's purpose.

Through the years of travelling and teaching people of His love, He lives in *hope* of His disciples understanding His messages and *hopes* that they will continue to teach His ways. He also remains in *hope* for humankind to love one another. Jesus knows He is unsettling ancient traditions even though He only comes to love the people.

Suffering enters His life through their fear of a reprisal by the authorities due to His controversial teachings. More *suffering* comes through His disciples' betrayal, denial, and abandonment of Him and His knowledge that the people plot to kill Him. He *survives* their rejection and *suffers* the *loss* of His own followers at His arrest.

In His agony, He calls to His Father to take His *suffering* from Him. He feels the *loss* of His mother and His beloved disciples at the foot of the cross. Through His death, He trusts and *believes* His Father, and through His resurrection, He becomes His soul in heaven. He shows us the way through life and death on earth and teaches us the only way of becoming our souls is to pass through these *seven steps* He lived.

During our lifetimes, each of us, in our own unique way, will replicate these seven steps to eventually becoming our souls. Our silence develops in childhood before we have a voice. Depending on the adults and individual circumstances chosen for our life, we can develop through this stage and become somewhat integrated into life.

There can, however, be complications in our development, such as sickness or disabilities in childhood; loss and grief of loved ones; poverty, addiction, war or death. Silence can also come through parental authoritarian control; child abuse in physical forms, such as beatings, neglect, abandonment; or verbal abuse, such as cruel words and lies; emotional abuse, such as manipulations and cruel mind games, withdrawal of love; and sexual abuse by parent/s, family, friends, or others.

In adulthood, this silence which has been created can develop into further abuse in our relationships, either by us or by others to us. This abuse comes in forms of suppressed silence, which becomes rage. It can result in domestic violence and deprivation of human liberties. These denied liberties can include access to our own relatives, food, shelter, finances; physical violence such as beatings, rape or homicide.

Throughout silence, other stages such as hope, suffering, and loss occur intermittently as we go from believing and hoping it will stop, and suffering and loss again when it doesn't. Survival is essential. These stages can oscillate throughout years of unawareness of how to get out of the situation and fear that you will escalate the violence further.

Anyone who has survived any of these events will know that it is during silence, hope, suffering, and loss that painful lessons of suppression of anger or rage and depression of feelings and thoughts can develop into disease. The silence may continue a lifetime, and release of the soul may occur through the tragedy of a tormented death. However, survival lessons of resilience, courage, forgiveness, strength of willpower, acceptance, and unconditional love can be learnt as we become our soul through these seven steps.

This story begins as a new soul arrives on earth to learn the lessons she has chosen for this lifetime. As a child she experiences her steps by her silence; in her hope; through her suffering; in her loss; and throughout her survival of abandonment, abuse, loss, and her withdrawal into her soul.

As a mother, she experiences her steps of silence, hope, suffering, loss, and survival as she comes to believe her soul, but she buries its profundity deep inside herself as she grieves the painful losses of her beloved ones. Throughout the story of becoming soul, she believes she not only heals her own grief but travels through time and heals generations of grieving in those she believes walks her journey with her. She continues her own unique seven steps to heaven by choosing to remain on earth to guide others in their own journey through their seven steps to heaven to becoming soul.

PART 1

Silence

1

Leaving Home

THE SOUL ENTERS THE ROOM, WHICH is flooded with intense light. A gasp tries to escape as the soul encounters a magnificent being of resplendent light. This being of light leads the soul to many other luminaries robed in magnificent, incandescent, white light. These luminaries observe the soul's arrival as they deliberate around a huge table. The soul is ushered by them in silence to present at their table. It's impossible for the soul to identify them as male or female.

With slow, deliberate movement, the soul approaches and stands in front of them. Mystified by an intense beam of light emanating from them, the soul feels intense scrutiny by each astounding individual. Only this moment exists for the soul.

In silence, they reveal that the soul is "of them."

A strange familiarity confuses the soul's awareness as it feels their warmth and acceptance of the stunned arrival. They continue their silent communication as the soul's inner vision expands into extensive realms. What the soul is hearing and experiencing resonates within as truth. Through their guidance, the soul chooses to analyse these thoughts and feelings.

The soul is seeing and experiencing all choices made during the lifetime just completed. The impact on others affected by the choices is also felt. Within their enclosed sanctuary, the soul aligns perceptions into reality and grasps the extent of wisdom remaining to be attained.

With humility and honour, the soul accepts the wise ones' instructions to "go and bring home the children." Another lifetime on earth for the soul to vanquish existing self-condemning thoughts and actions now exists.

Eagerness to begin again is irrepressible in the soul, and the rush to create new life tasks is essential. The choice is once again to master these new tasks by following the seven steps of silence, hope, suffering, loss, survival, belief, and heaven. These steps are given to each soul in accepting a new life.

Another parting gift of support and companionship is offered to the soul by the conclave of luminaries who have been assisting the soul since the arrival home. They finalise their audience with the soul with these silent words: "Our perpetual and silent communication is bestowed upon you."

The being of light, known as the Goddess, offers her gift last. In silence, she communicates to the soul, "I'll meet you in many forms throughout this new lifetime, together with the attending luminaries. It will depend on you to recognise me with them and accept or decline our servitude."

The power in the room is palpable with intoxicating passion fusing together with the Goddess's energy of light. Her essence of roses enhances as she eventually fades from the sanctuary with more silent words to the soul. "Find and take with you throughout your new lifetime the little black purse that you will find in a small alcove at the back of an old kitchen. It sits waiting to be found by you. You will need it on your journey."

These comforting directions that are given to the soul make the striding to the large main entrance and prising open the unshackled door easier. Before stepping through the huge exit, the luminaries silently introduce Sentel to the soul.

"Sentel is to be your companion and has gone before you to earth. He is to warn, protect, and keep you safe."

Sentel appears to the soul in a vision standing in the doorway and reaching out to the soul to forewarn, "Please don't go out there. The children! The children!"

Confusion takes hold in the soul's awareness as the choice to go back is to bring the children home. Without the soul fully understanding, Sentel opens the door wide to allow the vision to expand into a vast, open, and devastated landscape. Skeletal adults and children are wandering like the nearly dead. Others lie silently with open wounds, dying prostrate on the ground with the dust soaking up their own blood and bodily fluids among the already dead.

Sentel has no explanation and vanishes.

The intense suffering ricochets through the energy field of the soul's awareness as an extreme and tangible entity. The soul solemnly contemplates the warning while standing on the precipice and looking out across the wide expanse.

As the portal opens in front of the soul, acceptance of the daunting tasks that lay ahead for the soul is given to the conclave. The new life on earth is confirmed. Silence echoes back to the soul as the words are spoken. "As you leave here, your memory of who you are will fade. You will not remember what tasks you have set. It's your goal to search in each of your experiences while on earth for the lessons to be gained."

Intense energy surges forward through the narrow channel. Examining the crossing ahead, the move out into the swirling vastness by crossing the threshold into the transporting energy stream begins the journey for the soul.

The soul is unaware of any forewarning. There is no return. There is no fear.

Within the fluidity, the soul experiences the sensation of floating. Travelling passes as in a coma, and in this deep trance, the soul begins to become form. Continuous changes occur to this form throughout the voyage until eventually the fluid space becomes confined and uncomfortable. The form struggles to move, and the need to stretch is paramount.

Then without warning, the exit of the portal opens. The new form feels immense pain traversing into a strange, new stratosphere with a thunderous force. Upon the arrival, there is a compulsion to inhale the intoxicating ether to survive. A gulp, then a breath, then a scream as the eyes split apart and the full blast of a different intense light circulates and provokes a series of unpleasant and extreme sensations.

Through exhaustion, the new form lapses into unconsciousness. This darkness soothes the form, taking it into the previous trance. There are no memories of the journey.

Remaining in and out of consciousness and between distress and comfort, the new form of the soul tries to comprehend this new illusive environment, including its inhabitants, its odours, its noises, and its stillness. The darkness and the light both confound the thoughts. Tender experiences resonate and compete with tremendous fear. All these encounters become locked in the form as cellular retentions.

The struggle with grunts and moans to communicate to misunderstandings and the use of tears and wails to be understood is exhausting. The dark is reassuring of safety, and the light is bothersome.

A new child has arrived on earth. The soul has chosen the time of the new child's arrival when the earth is experiencing the chaotic post years of World War II. The new child will live in a small country town in Australia with a nearby city that carries the scars of the war.

It will grow in an environment of broken families with the loss of sons and daughters, but especially with children without fathers, mothers, brothers, and sisters. It will meet up with displaced persons and war-weary returning soldiers who are tormented, dismembered, and permanently wounded.

The arrival is at a time in earth's history when there is so much blood already spilt into the ground. So many lives of adults and children have been taken by warfare, forced internment, starvation, torture, and gas chambers.

During this time, many displaced persons come and settle where the child will live. They have chosen a country that is as far away from the war zones as possible. Healing is needed, and through example, the soul will become accustomed to reaching out to care for others throughout this life.

The child learns to respond to her name, Asina, and learns she has the form of a female, and her close significant others also have this form. She understands through experience what she's to do and what she's not to do. Growing, changing, and gathering endless instructions and using words are gruelling tasks.

Today is another morning in her young life, and Ralia stirs in her bed beside her. Both children belong to Ezara. Together they make their way to the kitchen, laughing and giggling while longing to see their mother. On their way, they pass a little black purse on the dresser at the back of the kitchen. Asina carries the purse for Ezara when they go to the marketplace, her favourite destination.

The marketplace brims daily with buyers and sellers and many stalls overflowing with freshly picked produce from surrounding farms. The three females wind their way through the fragrances of the various fruits and vegetables and meats and cereals that stimulate their senses and appetites. Each piece of fruit is polished until its skin shines and placed high upon the ever-growing pyramids of fruit. The glossy fruit catches the light of the day as the sun moves from east to west across the marketplace.

The bloodied red meats hang from hooks placed high above the sawdust-covered stone floors. Below, round chopping blocks stand high on wooden legs like ancient gnarled warriors carved by heavy knives and deeply gouged by the continuous hacking of meat and bones.

Ezara chooses cheap cuts of meat. The butcher chops through the bones with a well-worn axe and slices the meat into single serves. He wraps them in paper and gives them to Ezara. She places a loaf of freshly baked bread, which is still warm to the touch, atop the basket of meat, fruit, and vegetables, and they head for home.

Ralia and Asina run ahead of her, each with a handful of sweets given to them by a generous seller. It's easy to find the way home along the well-trodden path. Each smell, sight, taste, touch, and sound of the day, along with each stone and small crevice, becomes a memory etched in Asina's mind.

The girls hop and skip along the rugged path as Ezara waddles behind them while carrying the basket of goods she will prepare for dinner. Ralia stops to carry the heavy fruit for her. Asina manages to keep herself upright without falling and grazing her knees. The day will come when she will be able to carry the heavy basket for Ezara.

Just before the sun goes down, Ralia and Asina are sent to gather wood from the surrounding bush near the river for the oven fire. Ralia carries Asina on her back when she stumbles to keep up with her. She places Asina on her feet to gather small sticks that they poke at the crawling creatures as they try to escape back into their holes. They gather as many scratches as berries, as they collect the berries to eat on their way home with the load of wood. Together, they throw stones into the river as they follow its banks back home.

Ezara lights the fire and begins each evening meal preparing her fresh produce. As the last light of day disappears, the three pray at the table together in thanksgiving for food, shelter, and love. They eat their fill and all clean up together after the meal.

One warm bath is prepared for all of them to use. Asina is first, then Ralia. Ezara pours more hot water from the kettle from the stove top into the soapy water so she can at least enjoy the warmth of the used water. The girls are in their beds before she finishes.

Ezara sits alone near the fading coals of the open fire while the two wriggle themselves to sleep. They listen to her humming her songs as she mends their clothes. The clothes she makes late into each night. Each piece of cloth is shaped with love into dresses, shorts and shirts. Each piece of yarn is woven and knitted into winter jackets, hats, gloves, cardigans and blankets.

Her ancient hands are never idle from cooking, cleaning, creating, grooming, and hugging Ralia and Asina and her cat named Pet that curls up each night on her lap near the fire. The children's young lives are contented and predictable.

2

ᴏ℟hildhood

T HE RIVER IS THE LITTLE GROUP's place to relax. Ezara and the two
children fish and play there almost every day. It's summer and Asina
walks with them in the hot sun. She keeps cool by paddling at the water's
edge on their way to the markets for fresh food. She enters farther into
the water to grab at a floating stick. She misses the stick and stumbles,
then falls, then flounders in water too deep for her little body to stand in.

Ezara and Ralia are unaware of Asina at this moment and are walking
together nearby. They don't see her as she sinks into the dark water
behind them. Asina is alone as she gulps the water into her body. She
struggles as her breathing stops.

She remembers and she calls for the being of light. Instantly, she's
with the Goddess, who comforts her until she's at peace. Asina is so
excited to be with the Goddess. With such softness, the Goddess whispers
to Asina, "You aren't finished."

Asina is confused. Her memory of Ezara and Ralia is no more. She's
only aware of this moment with the beautiful Goddess of the light.

"I'm here! I'm here!" Asina replies excitedly.

The Goddess assures Asina, "You aren't finished. You must go back."

Asina is stunned. She feels this means separation and hardship. She
doesn't want to leave. She's content being home.

The Goddess is firm and insists she must return.

Asina decides to obey her Goddess. "I will go back," she hesitatingly
replies.

Asina instantly remembers Ezara and Ralia and sees their sadness
watching over her body in the hospital. Eerie sounds break the silence
and stillness between her and the Goddess. Asina is distraught as the light
of the Goddess subsides into the darkness.

Asina is jolted awake from a deep sleep. Her body aches. She doesn't
know where she is. The light of the room, people, tubes, and monitors
surround her. She sees Ezara and Ralia near her crying. They keep saying

to her, "You're back! We're here!" Asina drifts back to sleep. She rests for the day in hospital with them beside her. On the second day, she's ready to go home.

That night after the children's bathing and dinner are over, Asina goes into Ezara's room and sleepily climbs into her mother's bed to wait for Ezara to come to her side. Ezara holds Asina's hand that's clutching the rosary beads as they say a decade of the rosary together, a habit that often continues throughout Asina's childhood.

Drifting to sleep beside Ezara, Asina remembers the Goddess of the light. She aches to be with her. The Goddess comes and comforts Asina as she gives in to sleep while listening to Ezara mumble the rest of the rosary prayers.

Morning light appears as Asina awakens, hearing the birds in the trees singing in the sunrise. She feels warm and comfortable. She stretches her little body out till her toes touch the bottom of the bed. The chill awakens her warm feet and creeps up her legs. She hears Ezara up lighting the fire and preparing breakfast.

Asina kicks off the top cover, ready for the day, until she recalls the incident of drowning, the fear, and then the last gulp of air as the water rushed into her lungs, then silence. Her body shudders back under the covers. She calls out to her mother until Ezara answers her. Asina is comforted to hear her voice and gets up and goes to the kitchen. She rests all day close by Ezara and Ralia.

After a week, routine starts to fall back into Ezara's home with the remnants of the near-death incident diminishing. However, the deep longing in Asina to return to the Goddess is not diminishing.

Both Ezara and Ralia stay close to her as their fears have been unravelled. They both find at times Asina seems to wander off in her mind and appears to be talking to another person who isn't there in the room. Asina talks as though she's conversing with someone who she's very close to and knows intimately. She laughs and giggles with this imaginary person.

"Who is she talking to?" Ralia asks her mother.

Ezara replies, "It's her Goddess who's come to visit her. I think she's brought an angel with her this time."

Ralia doesn't understand. Her mother explains, "Angels and guides remain to protect and comfort those who experience a close death."

"Do I have an angel to protect me?"

"Yes, Ralia, I believe you have a guardian angel too. I believe we all do," Ezara explains to her as Ezara realises that Asina has returned with a close contact with her guardian angel.

Both Ezara and Ralia are relieved that Asina has company and support other than them to help her come through the trauma, and her mother encourages Asina to talk to and remain close to her angel. At night, the Goddess of the light is with her.

Asina is now in the two worlds of her belonging simultaneously.

Each day, Ezara and Asina walk Ralia to school as usual, and Asina can't wait to fetch her home again in the afternoons. When Ezara rests for her afternoon nap, the two girls go on adventures inside the house.

After Ezara's day cooking, Ralia lifts young Asina up to reach Ezara's biscuit tin placed high atop the kitchen dresser that holds her little black purse, which carries all that Ezara owns. Asina grabs the tin. Ralia puts her down on the floor while her fingers grapple to open it. They sneak a handful each of fresh sweet biscuits and return the tin to its place the same way they took it down. They dash to hide under Ralia's bed to finish off their spoils. Ezara knows their ways and lets them think that they make it clear of her.

Ralia has made friends with the neighbouring children. Some days, she climbs over their high fence which sides onto Ezara's little rented bungalow while Asina sits and watches them through the wire. There are many children in the family, and their mother, Larone, is a very close friend of Ezara.

Ralia plays with the children who are close to her own age, while Keren, the smallest child, comes to the fence, offering Asina her doll through the hole in the wire. Asina, being the same age, runs to get a doll Ezara made for her to show Keren.

Ezara stirs from her rest as Asina runs through the door. She realises the two children are outside. She comes to see what they are doing and watches Asina and Keren sharing their dolls. Larone soon appears, and the women chat while the children play. Asina becomes fearful as she intuits from her mother that all isn't well on the other side of the fence by the way the two women speak in hushed and serious tones.

Staring through the wire fence at the ancient home, she sees the many splattered toys strewn across the roaming verandas wrapping around the home. Compared to Ezara's little home, their house is too enormous for the child to comprehend.

Asina is excited that her circle of significant people is growing. She goes to the fence to play with Keren often, and she soon learns to climb the tall fence with Ralia and meets the children in her family. Larone treats them like her own, and the girls play alongside her as she works hard washing the mountain of clothes, sweeping the floors, and cleaning the outside play areas. She is kind and gentle, and often allows Asina and Ralia to play after school with the children before the girls gather the wood.

Ralia is with Ezara eleven years, and Asina is with her for nearly five years. Life is full, simple and settled. Ezara and the children are happy.

Early one morning, a stranger arrives at Ezara's bungalow. Ezara watches his approach as he meanders along the river edge and makes his way cautiously towards her closed gate. She is anxious as he slowly opens the gate. She moves away from the window and moves slowly to the door. He knocks, she hesitates, then she slowly opens it to him. She seems to know him and talks with him a long time outside on the porch before she asks him to come in.

Ezara comes to sit on the couch beside Ralia and Asina as they play on the floor. She introduces the man to the children, and they follow Ezara's lead to say hello. He takes his seat on the chair beside the couch. Asina gets up and leaves the room. Ralia is silent on her own. She doesn't understand what's happening. She hasn't seen him before.

Asina returns with her doll and finds that Ralia and Ezara are going for a walk with the man without her. Asina complains loudly.

Ezara leaves Ralia with him and comes back to Asina.

"You can't go with them. We must wait for their return here."

After an hour or so, Ralia comes back into the house on her own. She seems confused as she tells Asina about her time with him. "We walked to the river and threw stones in the water, and then we walked to the marketplace, and he bought me an ice cream."

Asina is now very upset. "Why couldn't I have gone too and had an ice cream?"

Both girls have no answers, and they are left only with their own strange sense of wanting to know more. Ezara gives the girls no further information and life goes back to normal.

Nearly a year passes, and there's another visit. Ralia spends time with him again leaving Asina on her own with Ezara.

Asina asks her mother, "Who is he?"

She tries to explain to the little girl the complicated story of Ralia's beginnings, but Asina doesn't understand. She doesn't start to become curious until, unexpectedly, after a further visit, Ezara surprises Asina by telling her, "Ralia is to leave us."

Something breaks in Asina's chest as she watches her sister and her mother become anxious and fearful over the following days and weeks. She sits with them to try to understand. To her, Ralia looks like she's floating out in space somewhere. One minute she's acting normal, and then she's empty and gazing into the distance.

Asina's afraid she's losing Ralia. She's afraid of losing Ezara too as her skin is white and cold to touch, like she's dying. She remembers that Pet went cold when he was dying.

Asina sees that one moment Ezara is in a panic and wants to run away with both children and starts packing all their clothes. Then she sits down and sobs and unpacks them. She has nowhere to go.

Asina sees that she's like Pet, trapped and waiting to die. Silence envelops the little family.

PART 2

Hope

3

Changes

THE CHILDREN'S YOUNG LIVES ARE NO longer contented and predictable. The little family has been shattered into a million pieces like glass as it hits the stone floor. Asina believes no one will be able to fix them.

The days are speeding on until Ralia leaves. All three are inconsolable in their silence and suffering. There's no hope left. The day before Asina's birthday is the day that Ralia is to leave them. Asina doesn't understand, and nothing is ever explained to her in a manner that she can understand. Ezara is distressed. Yet with a matter of fact voice, she tells the children what's going to happen next.

"We're to take Ralia to a strange distant city. You'll go with him from there, Ralia. Asina and I will come home."

Asina is hysterical and yelling, "No! No!" Falling to the floor, she screams "She is ours! Ralia stays here with us!" From her child's perspective, Asina has no comprehension of what's happening, other than fear and pain.

Ralia is sombre and silent. She hugs Asina and, choking on her tears, says, "I don't want to go."

Asina cries, "How can you leave us? You belong with Mumma and me!"

As evening presses in, like three wounded birds, they try to fly together. They eat the meal Ezara puts on the table. They clean up, bathe, and go to bed. Not one of them sleeps during the long night.

As planned, Ezara, Asina, and Ralia get out of bed early. They meet a cold winter's morning and rug up in warm clothes. They eat a small breakfast, pack plenty of food, and leave home to walk to the station. They arrive with Ralia's few belongings in plenty of time to catch the interstate train.

Their faces are drawn and gaunt and resemble the grey sky above them which is keeping the heavy mist tight to itself preventing any first rays of sunshine from shining through to the encased township.

15

They make their way to the booth to buy their tickets. It appears they're the only passengers travelling this early in the morning from the tiny hamlet. Ralia's luggage sits neatly on the platform by itself, waiting for their next movement, while the children huddle close to their mother, not daring to let go of her hands.

Right on the hour, the engine pulls into the station, dragging a multitude of carriages behind. As the train reaches distant townships and small cities along the way during the day and night, the empty carriages will become full of travellers before arriving in the state's capital.

Asina and Ralia sit next to each other with pencils and paper to keep themselves busy. They use their suitcases to lean on to draw and colour as the scenery whisks by their windows without them even noticing.

However, Ezara watches each scene as it appears framed through her window. Inside the frame, visions of Ralia as a baby, a toddler, a school child, and as she glances at Ralia, she sees her how she is now. Her mind feels as though it can't hold onto one thought. It jumps from distant thoughts of Ralia growing bathed in her love to a young girl soon reaching pubescence sitting beside her waiting to meet a family she doesn't know.

Ezara feels there's something dying inside her and her locked-up emotions aren't even trying to come out. She's committed to delivering her child into strangers' hands without trying to resist. The incongruence in her mind drains her mental energy. It doesn't seem feasible to her that she'd be doing such a thing to Ralia.

Hours pass slowly, and the young girls are wriggling and fidgeting. Their mother pulls out the food she cooked and packed into a picnic basket. Sandwiches and fruit and a small cake for each of them make them feel they're enjoying the trip. Ezara pulls out the thermos of hot tea and pours some into a tin travelling cup for herself. She opens another flask of warm chocolate milk for the girls. For a moment, all seems well again. The same procedure is repeated during the day until it's time to sleep.

Blankets and small pillows are shared to make themselves as comfortable as possible. Many trips to the toilet happen through the night as well as bouts of stretching and resettling in awkward positions to try to become comfortable again.

Tired and exhausted, the three travellers arrive at their destination in the early morning, with wide eyes and overwhelming trepidation. They step off the train onto the city platform and make their way to public transport to get them to the planned meeting place. It's as if their emotions have frozen in time as they arrive at the city square. They walk to a bench seat and sit and wait. The noise of traffic and people resound in their ears. They scan faces of passers-by, searching for the familiar face.

They've been waiting for nearly an hour and anxieties have worsened when the person they're waiting for arrives from behind them. They startle. Initial greetings are difficult and short. Further conversation is stunted and prolonged. Then silence permeates the air.

He reaches out to Ralia to come to him.

She hesitates and grabs Ezara's hand.

Ezara turns sideways away from Ralia. She knows Ralia is to leave. She needs to let go now.

Ralia grabs Asina as Ezara lets her go. Ralia reverberates with an excruciating shriek as she screams into Asina's ear, "No, I'm not going!"

A tussle ensues. Held by the arm, she's lifted out of Asina's reach and carried off.

Ralia screams for Ezara, "Mumma! Mumma! Mumma!"

Ezara sobs and begins to run to Ralia.

Ralia disappears.

Asina runs to Ezara screaming, "Mumma! Mumma! Mumma!"

Ezara falls to the ground, sobbing. Asina falls on top of her. Together, they merge into one groaning distortion of humanity. Sweat droplets appear on their faces amidst the tears. Silence and pain controls.

Ezara scoops Asina up into her lap. Their bodies and souls grieve the loss deeply as they cling together. Hours seem to pass by as they sit on the ground alone in a foreign city. Time has no meaning to them.

When the need to toilet and eat is urgent, Ezara gathers Asina up, and they search for these essential needs. Ezara drags Asina along. Asina drags Ezara along. Food is bought to take on the journey home.

The last train for the day is boarded, and Ezara hugs Asina to herself and softly sobs into her long, black hair. No joy is had when they eat their food without Ralia, and no fun is exacted while settling into sleep. As the light of day turns to darkness, Asina falls asleep and stays in her mother's embrace for the long journey home.

Once again, the Goddess of the light is with her with many luminaries shining in her light. She holds Asina and soothes her with unspoken words. She calms. Asina just wants to go home with the Goddess. Her heart is in pain.

The sun of the next day is setting behind the mountains of home as the train stops in their little town. Ezara gently wakens Asina. They walk the last part of their journey in the late-afternoon darkness in silence.

Ezara opens the door of the house, knowing Ralia is not there. Asina goes to Ralia's bed, which is made neat and tidy with her few unwanted belongings still sitting on the pillow just as she left it. She turns to find her birthday presents wrapped in pretty butterfly paper sitting on her own pillow. She rushes to Ezara to open them together. One is from Ralia.

The nightly chores of cooking dinner and baths are soon over. Ezara lights the candles of the cake, turns off the lights, and sings softly to Asina. Their exhaustion in their bodies is felt as they fall into their beds. To sleep without Ralia beside her is daunting to Asina, so she crawls into bed with her mother. There, she falls into a deep sleep with the knowledge that Ralia is no longer here. The ache in her chest is unbearable. Her angel comforts her through the night.

Days, then weeks, disappear. Ezara and Asina have become silent about Ralia. They have no way to contact her. She doesn't contact them.

Ezara gazes off into the fire as the coals turn into embers each night. She walks to the front gate every morning as if she's taking Ralia to school, and she waits at the gate every afternoon with Asina for Ralia to come home from school.

She leaves Ralia's few baby belongings on the bed and in her cupboard. Her photo remains in Asina's hands. Asina is lost. She feels her mother's needs but doesn't know how to help her.

Months disappear, simply surviving, and Asina feels she's now beginning to become Ezara's focus again. She starts school, but she's so reluctant to go. Ezara drags her each day along the stone path and she leaves her inside the school gate each morning. The separation is unbearable for both.

Asina cries for her all day until her mother comes for her in the afternoon. They walk to the markets on the way home. Asina carries the little black purse. No longer does she skip along the path. She carries Ezara's basket of food home.

Alone, Asina gathers the wood and has the first bath. She lies alone in her bed as Ezara finishes in the kitchen and bathes. Asina no longer hears her mother singing her favourite songs.

Asina sits in the pew beside Ezara at church each Sunday without Ralia. She sees the angels in the small country church painted on the walls. They converse with her in silence. She's never alone. Kindness appears in the form of caring nuns at school and understanding neighbours next door.

Keren is a friend she goes to when she misses Ralia. She climbs the fence, and they play together. Asina learns to be content with Keren, who tries to replace Ralia and with the ever-presiding light beings in the new realm she visits each night. Each day, she grows more loved by Ezara, who is aware that there's an open wound within their souls.

Asina becomes closer to Ezara on her own until someone else new arrives and changes her world. Ezara's married daughter, Siroda, who has been away for many years, returns. She is living in a nearby city. Asina knows nothing of her.

Although Asina realises her mother's heart is more content now, Siroda is back and she has become involved in her life again. Over time, Asina gets to know Siroda and her husband, Gus, a returned soldier who was wounded in battle, when she visits with Ezara.

Asina develops a relationship as a younger sister with Siroda who tends to develop a sibling rivalry with Asina in relationship with Ezara. Asina learns she needs to love Siroda because Ezara loves Siroda. Her life has become complicated, although when not in their company, Asina revels in her life with Ezara by herself.

Since their arrival, Asina goes alone to the markets for Ezara, walking on her own from school. She walks the same cobbled path and follows the river and collects the wood to light the fire. Life has somehow lost happiness for Asina. She worries about her mother as it seems that Ezara is always on her bed lately. She sees her mother is not well.

Siroda also knows her mother is not well and comes to Asina and tells her, "You need to come and live with me as you are too much for Ezara now."

Asina doesn't understand until Ezara goes into hospital and Siroda and Gus take her home with them. They put her in a new school which she needs to bus to and from each day on her own. Gus is always at work in his own business, and Asina becomes Siroda's helper with their young children.

Asina and the children and Gus and Siroda are all living together in a small house in a suburb in the city, sharing bedrooms and belongings. Asina finds this arrangement intolerable and the full house stifling and longs to go back to her mother.

Ezara is recuperating in hospital after a major operation, and when it is time for her to leave, she comes to stay with Siroda until she's well enough to go to her own home. Asina thrives with her there, knowing she will be going home with her soon. She feels her mother's warm presence in the home and goes off to school content, knowing Ezara will be there when she comes home.

A month passes slowly, and Ezara is up and trying to help Siroda with a few light chores. Asina is relieved to see her mother becoming her old self again. Instead of sitting on the end of the bed to visit with her, Asina finds Ezara out in the garden sitting in the shade of an old tree when Asina gets home from school. It's only a few more weeks, and her mother has fully recovered and prepares to go home.

It's then that Ezara tells Asina, "You won't be going home with me. I think it is better for you to stay with Siroda and the family." Asina is shocked and begins to cry. She feels abandoned, and once again, her heart breaks. Asina didn't return to live with her mother permanently when Ezara left Siroda's.

Ezara has shown her child how to shop, cook, wash, and clean and how to make and mend clothes. She has also shown her how to do the chores for Siroda and her family.

Each night, after all her chores are done for Siroda, Asina removes herself from the family to be alone in her part of the bedroom she shares.

She builds an emotional wall around herself by creating a shrine to her Goddess on her wall beside her bed. She immerses herself more and more into the spirit realm and when going to sleep she wraps herself in the comfort of her Goddess. She arises early each morning and walks the hour journey to and from the church for daily Mass on her own, arriving home in time to catch the bus to school.

4

Future

E ZARA COMES BACK AND FORTH EACH week to Siroda's home, and Asina can't wait for her arrival. She stays with the family for two or three days and always takes Asina home with her each weekend. Gus collects Asina each Sunday night to go back to school to her friends and the nuns.

Asina trusts the nuns and is open with them, sharing her pain with them. They know Asina has become withdrawn and deeply emotional, and they've comforted her at school, realising that she's fretting for her mother and has found it difficult to settle since she left without her. Asina loves helping them clean the church and put flowers on the altar. She feels so close to Jesus and the Goddess when she's in their home. Asina becomes so close to the nuns that she decides she just wants to be just like them when she gets older.

Asina's life becomes more fragmented and confusing for her, and she spends many hours on her own feeling displaced and alone. She withdraws further into herself, and more and more, she grows to love the time she spends in company with her Goddess and angels. She eagerly waits to sit with Ezara in the church each Sunday to feel them. It's through these times that she decides this is where she wants to be for the rest of her life.

Asina talks to the Goddess, pleading with her to fill her empty heart. Siroda has another child who brings new life and hope to the lonely teenager. Study crowds out any other heaviness or lightness for Asina. As she attends high school in the city and travels by bus on her own, she can make the decision to travel back to Siroda each day or catch a bus that will take her to Ezara. Asina chooses to go to her sickly and aging mother to be able to spend more time with her as she always wanted.

The Mother Superior tells Asina that she needs to be in the workforce for at least two years before they'll take her. Two years seems a long time, and her heart once again aches as she sits in the church focusing on the crucifix with an image of Jesus nailed to it. She absorbs the energy of the sacred place and feels the urgent call to work for Jesus so strongly in her soul. The pain of waiting in her soul is so tangible that she knows Jesus feels it too.

She walks out of the church and walks home to Ezara. She knows she can legally leave school and that she has eighteen months to go before she'll graduate with a high school certificate, but she has made up her mind to leave. Without asking or telling Ezara, she finishes her school years.

She tells her mother what she has done and what she wants to do. Ezara is shocked and upset that she has left school and wants to spend her life in a convent. Asina tries to tell her mother, "They aren't as strict as they used to be. I'll be travelling with other nuns, teaching country children about Jesus." This concept resonates fully with Asina's soul.

The idea of a two-year wait doesn't send her back to school as Ezara wants but sends her out into the workforce to gain experience until she's of the age that they will allow her to enter.

She seeks work with Gus, who creates an opportunity in his office for Asina to learn reception work and bookkeeping. She begins naive and inexperienced, working under the head of administration who befriends the young Asina.

She moves from his small business into a bigger corporation as a trained ledger operator in the business, and she has become one of the young ones among many in the office. She socialises with them, and she tells the interested young men of her one desire.

She's still staunch in her decision and has kept in touch and met up with the Mother Superior and is getting ready to enter. Asina knows Ezara is so unhappy with her choice.

Asina chooses to go to a social night with her young co-workers before she leaves the company. Walking behind her group, who are deciding who they're travelling with and whose car they're each travelling in, Asina decides she'll go with anyone in any car available. She's aware of others going to the event wandering slowly behind her. A strong hand grabs her arm, and she's offered a ride. She looks behind to see Sentel, who she barely knows. A light twinkling in his eyes catches her attention and his incandescent smile indicates to her that he's sincere. She doesn't think; she just agrees to go with him.

Her life changes in that moment. They spend the social together and stay within the group, and he drops her home. He asks to be her friend. She tells him of her plans and how close it is before she leaves.

"That's okay by me," Sentel tells her. Asina is puzzled by his interest in her.

She agrees and learns Sentel is five years older and lives with his family. He tells her his father is the son of a Christian pastor who escaped from Europe during the war years to their country town, leaving behind family survivors of the carnage. He won't see them again throughout his lifetime.

Sentel's mother is the daughter of a farming family and works hard to keep her family together on their farm. She's one of the suppliers of fresh produce to the markets Ezara frequents. Asina realises Sentel separates himself from any domestic dramas and has become a loner in his family.

Sentel becomes interested in Asina's plans and accompanies her on her routine of daily prayer services. To Asina's surprise, Sentel begins to embrace his own inner voice to expand his call as a Christian, something his father didn't carry on from Sentel's grandfather. Asina feels his grandfather leading him on from the spirit world to find his soul.

Asina tries to continue her journey, but each time she tries to follow her chosen path, she senses a strange stirring of memories when she's with Sentel. He is familiar.

Sentel sees Asina trying to come to terms with the decision for her life. He sees her communicate with her Goddess and with her beings of light. He knows she's different to other girls he's met. To be fair to her and give her space, he takes a transfer with his office and moves to another town to work. Living away on his own, he gathers a taste of Asina's independence and freedom.

Even apart, their lives expand together as they keep in contact with each other, and Sentel visits regularly. Asina attends Sentel's church service for his spiritual initiation and comes to realise she won't be leaving him. The souls of Asina and Sentel have bonded in spirit unaware of their souls' pasts or their earthly future together.

Ezara approves of Sentel as he's older and more conservative. Asina sees that her mother is more content now that she's not leaving her, at least not for a religious life in a convent. Sentel is kind to Ezara, and he learns to love her as Asina does.

Asina and Sentel come with their two children to stay with Ezara as she hasn't been well. Asina wakes to feed her children and takes Ezara a cup of tea. The two sit and talk as the sun opens the day. Both women are absorbed in talk of the future. Ezara knows her time left here is short, and she wants to be with Asina and her family as much as she can.

"Asina, I feel I need the hospital again," she says.

"This time, it isn't good, is it? You won't come home, will you?" Asina asks Ezara.

She lovingly replies, "Sentel and the children are to fill you now. I'm to go home." Asina cries softly on her mother's shoulder.

Ezara whispers, "I have something else to tell you, Asina."

"What, Mumma?" Asina listens intently.

"Siroda left you with me when you were born to her and Gus. She couldn't cope with Gus after he returned from the war. He needed time to recover. I tried to help, but she didn't want that kind of help from me. She left with Gus, and they went away for a long time. She has tried since she has come back. She's your mother. Go to Siroda. I'm your grandmother."

Asina doesn't want to hear it. She can't believe what Ezara is saying. It feels like her mother is abandoning her again and diminishing their relationship. She says to her mother firmly, "You are my mumma and always will be."

"You'll forget me Asina when I leave. You won't remember me. You have your own family now."

Asina gasps, "No, no, I'll never forget you." She feels shocked and lost.

She solemnly prepares Ezara's things for her to leave home for the last time. She leaves Sentel with the children and goes in the ambulance with Ezara. They hold hands together. They're bound by their love. Asina doesn't want to let go of her only mother, whom she wants to stay, just for her.

Days go by slowly but too quickly for Asina as she sits with her mother each day in the hospital. Siroda visits daily. Asina looks at Siroda differently now, but she only knows one mother.

Asina arrives at the hospital on Good Friday. She's physically struggling during these last six weeks before bearing her third child. There's no time for Asina to process what Ezara has told her.

Ezara is crying when Asina walks in the room. Asina reaches to wipe her mother's tears. Ezara can hardly speak now. She lies uncomfortably in her bed while Asina rubs her painful legs.

Ralia arrives early afternoon. Asina has called her to come. Ralia found them when she left home and married. She's a mother too now. She has been visiting Ezara for four or five years. The three of them are family again.

Siroda is called when Ezara asks for her medicine she knows will help her pass peacefully. She sits to the back of the room, sobbing. The sisters sit with their mother as they each know her.

Around 3:00 p.m., about the time it's said that Jesus took His last breath on the cross, a priest arrives and anoints Ezara with holy oils. During the ceremony, Asina lets out a heart-wrenching sob as the sound of a hundred trucks thundering by explodes in her ears. She watches Ezara as she looks out into the distance and smiles. Asina knows the angels and beings of light are preparing Ezara for her journey home.

Ralia leaves after the anointing. She can't watch anymore. She's as broken as she was leaving Ezara as a little child.

Night comes and Ezara says to Asina, "You go now."

"No, Mumma," Asina replies lovingly.

Ezara sleeps. Siroda waits outside. Asina waits beside her mother's bed.

At around 1:00 a.m. Easter Saturday morning, she releases Asina's hand. "I love you!" she whispers to Asina as she slips away peacefully. These are her last words to Asina. Asina doesn't cry. She just sits beside her mother till she needs to leave.

Outside, Asina takes Sentel's hand. They go to collect their children. Asina lies beside Sentel in the early morning light, realising no one else who was present at the anointing heard the noise. The Goddess comforts her and a light being explains to her, "That was the opening of the portal between heaven and earth that you heard with the angels at death coming to guide Ezara's soul home."

Asina sleeps.

The sun is fully risen in the sky before she wakes. She goes to make breakfast for her children and notices Ezara's little black purse, now unused, lying on the bench. Asina picks the purse up and holds it to her heart. It contains all her love and teachings. Ezara's love and teachings are now Asina's forever.

PART 3

Suffering

5

Challenges

Asina and Sentel welcome their third child, Neena, born six weeks after Ezara leaves. During the birth, Asina once again travels through the dark tunnel to the light, and a light being appears to tell her she must go back. She resists again, but it's of no use. She feels so wretched saying yes. All she wants is to be with Ezara. She awakens, and they lay her baby in her arms. She has dark hair and sallow skin like Ezara. Asina barely recalls the journey from which she just returned.

Each day, Asina finds her emotions of sadness and happiness chaotic as the children demand her attention constantly. Another challenge comes. They won't be able to stay in their two-bedroom rented house as the children grow. They'll need to save money to get a larger dwelling.

They decide that Asina will need to help earn an income, so they lease a small business in the town where they can take the children to work with them. By the time their fourth child arrives, they're ready to take a house loan and move into a larger home in the farming area. Ezara's words, "You will forget me," start to come to fruition as she works and raises the children. Asina hasn't grieved her mother or even brought her to mind.

Siroda has become distant and angry and isn't coping with losing her mother. Their youngest child is the only child left at home, and she's struggling at school and is emotionally troubled.

Asina has formed a close motherly bond with her young sister, and when they move into the larger home, Nica comes to live with them. She's the first of many distraught children who find their way to Asina and Sentel.

For Asina, life races forward with five children to care for, a business to run, and no time for Sentel to be with her other than at work. Her emotions are shoved down deeper and deeper, and Ezara becomes lost to her.

Gus and Siroda separate, and Nica resumes life with Siroda and begins her working life.

Their youngest child, Nettie, is three when large cracks in her family picture develop. Asina and Sentel are moving further and further apart, and the young children are missing family life. The need for change is evident, and Asina desperately tries to solve their troubles.

She lies each night in the dark before going to sleep, and her mind wanders back and forth over the life that she knows is falling apart. She feels abandoned and alone without any connections to family since Ezara left her behind. She has no one to talk to, and her deep emotions are blocked off to her.

Years later, Asina lies alone in the dark of the night, once more deeply pondering her family falling apart, at another turning point in their lives. She floats amongst her thoughts of Nettie as a little child. She believes Nettie is her little child of grace. The one who comes when she's told she can have no more children. The little one she protects from her older siblings' antics. The one who stays so close to her throughout her life. Asina wells up with tears but can't cry. She panics and calls in her Goddess of the light and her angel and guides for their support. They guide her soul as she travels far away from her wandering memories of Nettie's childhood, to once again experiencing Nettie's last hours of life with her.

She's sitting beside Nettie's bed, watching as her adult child's last breaths leave her body. She keeps a close vigil each day and night with Nettie as she journeys to her soul's release. She's constantly accompanied by the feeling of the futility of wanting her daughter to stay. This futility now causes her to squirm in the armchair that she has occupied during these long weeks and has again sent her to the visitors' lounge.

Arriving back thirty minutes later from having yet another coffee in the lounge, Asina opens Nettie's door to her one-bed hospital room. The nursing staff have left after adjusting her medication and wiping her body down. The last nurses' rounds before lights out is over. Nettie lies alone in a state of induced silence caused by the medication which has eased her pain but has left her unable to verbalise.

As Asina passes through the door, she enters a hot steamy energy which feels like she just opened the shower door. She walks towards Nettie, and once again, she passes through another identical energy on the left side of the bed. She deliberately walks to the right side of the bed, and it has the same high-energy flow. Asina knows that the angels, whom she has met several times before, are present with other spirits.

She walks to Nettie's left side and whispers in her daughter's ear, "They're here. Don't be afraid." Although she's in a semi-induced coma with the permanent morphine medication, tears seep through Nettie's closed eyes.

Asina hugs her child. She knows that it's painful for her to leave her children as well as her mother and family. Nettie has been a single mum for years and has received little to no support other than from her own family during this time and especially during her long illness. Asina holds her beautiful daughter's hand until she settles.

Asina silently speaks to the spirits. She begs for more time. She also asks them not to scare Nettie. "Please be gentle with her and don't frighten her as you did me the first time." Asina knows she's to pull back and let Nettie talk with them on her own.

Eventually, she lies down on the makeshift bed at the foot of Nettie's bed, the one that she's used during these past weeks. She knows Nettie is seeing others on the other side and experiencing heaven.

"You'll have all night with her," she hears the spirits whisper to her. Grateful, she tries to get a little sleep while Nettie is in their company. Asina knows this is the last time she'll lie here. Sadness and joy come to each of them.

During a broken sleep, Asina hears every sound Nettie makes. Asina hears Nettie's breathing. It's laboured. Asina gets up to sit by Nettie's side. Asina waits to hear another breath and when it comes, Asina relaxes a little.

Nursing staff attend to Nettie during the night. This is when Asina gets up and leaves for the lounge again. She sits and again reads all the signs and pamphlets before returning to Nettie. The night is long, but Asina doesn't want the sun to come up.

She again lies down and closes her eyes for a short time, and when she opens them again, daylight is breaking through the night's darkness. Nursing staff are again doing their rounds. They don't come to Nettie. Asina dashes to get a quick coffee to wake herself up and brings it back. On her return, she sees that Nettie has changed her breathing pattern again. Now, there are long spells between each breath. She sits beside Nettie and holds her cold hand. She can't believe that she's leaving. She is totally aware that these are their last moments together.

Separation from her diseased body comes with Nettie's last shallow exhalation. Asina waits for another breath. It doesn't come. She is finally released from her physical body.

Asina softly utters, "Oh no!" She doesn't cry. Silence permeates Asina's soul as she needs to close her thoughts to Nettie once again.

She eases the immediate pain of the loss of her child by opening her thoughts back to when she and Sentel hope they have found the solution to saving their relationship and young family.

They decide to sell their business and rent out the house and set off on a new adventure to live on a remote island. They love the idea and believe the time together will bring them closer as a couple and as a family.

They're so excited that they can lease a business and home there, and they'll be able to farm the land as well. They travel to inspect the area with the children and are soon on a high-speed seafaring vehicle smashing through the crests of waves and getting sprayed with cool seawater. The children are enticed into the new adventure easily.

Asina and Sentel are beaming with their choice of adventure and are sold on the way of life even before they put their feet on the island. They have visions of all becoming competent sailors who will learn the ways of the sea as they travel it regularly. Sentel can't wait to get in the captain's seat. Asina can't wait to excite the family with island living.

They move their belongings, and life resumes on the island. The children are homeschooled by Asina, and they learn to live together as their only playmates. The weather, the isolation, family life, the farm, the business, the old farmhouse, and the sea, all factor in "a day in the life of an islander."

Asina is up at sunrise each day feeding the chickens and Sentel milking the cows. The children are up completing their homework from yesterday's lessons. She feels at home amongst the excitements of the island's energies. Peace reigns again for Asina. Her little family is united and happy.

She and Sentel have built a little chapel at the back of the kitchen where she teaches the children to pray. They gather there each morning and night for bible stories and for their daily worries to be shared.

She asks the Goddess in the middle of early family prayer, "How do I teach my children faith?"

She hears the answer from the Goddess. "Be what you teach the children. Be love. Be kind. Be patient. Be understanding. Be gentle in your ways. Be forgiving. Be accepting. Be your soul."

"How do I become my soul?" Asina asks the Goddess.

Asina's conversation with the Goddess continues in the chapel while the children and Sentel leave to eat the breakfast warming in the wood fuelled oven.

The Goddess teaches her more deeply. "Faith takes the discipline of your mind, the integrity of your will, and God's blessings of grace for you to be able to bend your will towards believing in His love for you. Faith takes a truly humble and simple person to be able to bend their knee and bow their head to His ways. Replace worldly perceptions for His truths that are beyond human comprehension," she tells Asina.

The Goddess continues, "I want others to know my son, Jesus. I want you to tell them."

In hearing the Goddess's words "my son, Jesus," Asina realises that she's talking with the Mother of Jesus. She's overwhelmed in this moment of awareness. She contains the squeal of excitement and pure ecstasy! She hugs her chest to stop it from bursting from the explosion of pure joy. Tears well up in her eyes. She holds her head as if it's going to fly away.

Her head pounds with thoughts. *I'm talking with the Mother of Jesus! It's you who has come to me all my life to comfort me, mother me, and love me.* Asina exhales and takes a slower breath. Her Goddess is Mary and Her Son is Jesus!

Overwhelmed with the presence of the Holy Spirit, Asina hears Mary's words.

"Just as a child studies the world around them in silence, listen for the voice of spirit in the stillness that surrounds you in nature. Quieten your busy mind and sit with Him in silent prayer. Each night and morning listen to Him in silence. Stay in the silence you create in your mind and absorb the love and protection of those who love you.

"Always hope and pray, for without hope and prayer, there's no joy, no peace, no happiness. You know I'm always with you in your suffering and joy. Continue to call to me, and I'll come to you as I've done since you were a child.

"There's much suffering, loss, and grief in this life on earth, but you'll survive and come to believe. And you'll live in your soul, and you'll be set free.

"Share your home, belongings, and talents with others and be of help to people in need. If you share with others, Asina, you'll drink from the deep waters flowing from the well of life-giving waters."

Mary speaks a simple message to Asina, "Love Jesus with all your heart and soul."

Asina permeates Mary's essence throughout the coming days, weeks, months, and years that she spends on the island farm with her children. She's constantly enthused with passionate love and empathy for others. Abandoned children in need of her virtuous qualities are guided by Mary to her family.

Her introduction to Mary's children happens when the family see that visitors are mooring their boat off the old jetty and meandering their way up the sand track to the little picnic area that Asina and her family created for themselves when they first arrived on the island.

The family leaves breakfast to be kept warm as they go to greet the newcomers to the island. Asina and Sentel walk along the track and down the hill towards the beach with the children riding ahead on their bikes. The children usually ride down to the beach after their lessons each day to catch worms for bait for their fishing adventures on the incoming tides. They can catch up to twenty or thirty fish as quickly as they can pull them in if they can get to the right position in the right moment, and they're always prepared with bait for that moment.

As they get closer to the new visitors, they can see they have children with them. Asina's children are eager to meet them. As the two groups merge, a unique bond instantly develops. Both groups of children seem to reach out to each other. Asina welcomes the newcomers to the house for refreshments.

A kettle of water for a pot of tea is soon on the stove top, and the stove's receiving another log of wood on the live coals. Their breakfast is shared with the visitor's packed food. Adult talk ensues into lunch, and the children have found their own enjoyment elsewhere.

After lunch, the groups disperse, with visitors catching the tide home to the mainland and the island family beginning their afternoon chores of collecting wood for the fire, carrying water for bathing, and gathering vegetables from the garden to begin the night's meal.

Around the kitchen table at night, the stories of their guests of the day become the topic of discussion between the adults and the children. Asina tells the children, "The children are homeless, and the adults with them are their 'carers.' We are invited to become holiday carers and bring the children here for their holidays."

Asina tells the children that both groups of adults seemed delighted by the suggestion and left with plans to be made for the children to visit during the next school break. The children are surprised but seem satisfied with the idea and tentatively agree to the suggestion.

Before the holidays, Asina and her family visit the children on the mainland. Asina's children arrive very nervously with their parents and get their first-hand experience with children who don't live with their families. They become overwhelmed by the number of children who race out to meet them, and they look to their parents for reassurance. Children of all ages come out to meet them, some with toys they want to show them, some who want them to play with them. Others just come and touch them, but the children all have the same desperate look in their eyes of needing a family to love them.

The family feels the need to show their best behaviour and attitudes during the visit, but meeting the children has weakened their resolve that they are even good enough for such a job. They feel depleted of the energy and the bravado that they first arrived with. It seems to the family that there isn't enough of them to share around to each child in need. They feel very exhausted and overpowered.

The children who came to their home are asked if they want to go with the family for the holidays. Their immediate and positive responses encourage Asina's children that they could share their parents with them. All are pleased that the children have shown such a favourable interaction. It's this bond with the children that helps the parents to agree to the proposition of becoming holiday carers.

The children race to get their belongings and are in the family car before anyone can find a reason to disagree with the decision. The drive through the city to the boat harbour seems to take a long, silent time as everyone is getting used to the strangeness of being or becoming members of the family.

Sentel parks the car in the rented garage at the harbour and walks back to the jetty to be with Asina and the children. They load the boat with belongings and extra food for the next two weeks and set off in the early afternoon to arrive home just before dark. The arrival is seamless, and the night meal is completed. They make their way to their beds on the first night together as an adventure that would equal any other adventure they are to have during the coming weeks.

6

Abandonment

HOLIDAYS ARE SHARED WITH MANY CHILDREN on their island home during the years. Asina and Sentel are contacted regularly when a child needs a holiday with the love and attention of the family. Asina's children have company coming and going in their lives constantly. Their hearts are opened to those in great need of love and acceptance, and this crucial life lesson of empathising with and accepting others is to infiltrate their childhood and into their adult lives.

When the island lease is nearing its end, Sentel is informed that no further lease is available. The family are devasted. The day of leaving is filled with great turmoil of uprooting the whole family. They've culled their belongings to make them fit onto the barge that's to leave on the early-morning full tide. Time is essential in getting all the belongings on the deck in the short time.

The barge pulls back from the shore as the tide is turning and rounds the pier and heads out. The family watches their island home disappear on the horizon for the last time as the barge slowly makes its way through the narrow passage of water and sandbanks and sails the family back to the mainland. Each member tears up and feels displaced as each large splash of water hits the front of the closed loading ramp on the barge. Memories flood their minds, watching the smooth waters glisten in the sun.

Asina feels the wrench from the good times of having sailed these waters during the years and knowing the taste of salt on their skin and heavy salt in their hair. They have seen many capsize their small boats in the uncertain waters. They've even been asked to look for missing bodies that may have washed up on the island shores. It feels like a long journey back to the mainland and "societal norms" for the family.

Sentel has hired a furniture truck to meet the barge at the other end of their final journey. Once the barge is unloaded, Asina drives the car with the children and their pets. Sentel drives the truck the long, slow journey to their home that's now vacant. On arrival, they unpack and set up as best as they can before night comes in. They fall onto their beds, exhausted, with dreams of their island home very vivid in their sleeping state. It's a time of great upheaval, and it's going to take a long time for each of them to become a mainlander again.

Their exhausting arrival and a disturbed sleep are shared by all. Asina is up at sunrise to make breakfast. The next job of the day is to contact the local school to enrol the children. Books and uniforms will need to be organised, and Sentel will start the day by immediately looking for work. The children unpack their belongings and set up their rooms. Their sadness of leaving their island home releases into anger. It will take time for them to grieve a way of life that nurtured their souls.

Sentel is meeting up again with one of his mates who offers him a job at the fruit markets. Asina knows that once again she needs to find paid work by finding another shop for them to lease.

With the shift off the island, holidays with other children cease. The children are in mainstream schooling for the first time in their lives, and they find it exhausting with the restrictions in the classroom. They feel the disruption in their learning by the constant noise and the lack of concentration of their peers. The children especially miss their very early morning lessons and their lunchtime finishes for extra adventures.

Asina finds it easier with all the children in school. She finds the touch of a switch to turn on a light, a switch to turn on the stove, and to access indoor water overshadows the chores of lighting the fire, gathering wood and carrying water. Being able to walk on carpet is a strange, tactile experience and having personal showers is a blessing. She spends the next weeks concentrating on establishing directions for their new life.

The family establishes a business and work together once more, settling into a new life on the mainland. Asina and Sentel become involved in youth work with their children through the local community, and they share great times with many young people. One day, a homeless teen who they've become close to seeks them out and asks to live with them. The family agrees, and life becomes full of students with homework, assignments, exams, holidays, and troubles.

It's only a matter of time before the teen packs all her belongings and leaves. After missing for days, a phone call tells Asina that she's not coming back. The family hears from her again when she comes back to give birth to her child with their support. She manages for a few months with Asina's help, then leaves the baby with the family. Lucah becomes a part of the family from his birth.

Lucah is in school when the older children are leaving home and heading for university in the city and when their last child is born. It becomes another time of great change in the family. It's then that Sentel begins to complain that the business is slowing down as well, and Asina knows they're struggling. Her response to the situation this time is, "I need to get an outside job!"

She moves to the city with the children and seeks financial assistance to study. She leaves Sentel working the business and trying to pay the house off without carrying the weight of the family.

Asina and Sentel realise the move causes great unrest in their relationship, and they find many unresolved issues between them that need attention. The time of separation between the couple gives them the opportunity to come to terms with unmet needs and to plan their future outcomes.

After a three-year separation, Sentel moves to Asina in the city and finds work. He sells the family home and the business to pay off any remaining debts and have a deposit for a new life with Asina. With her studies complete, Asina starts her own business. They move together to a new home and farm to start again.

Then as unexpectedly as Lucah arrived in the family, just as unexpectedly, his family comes back after nearly ten years and takes him to live with them. There's no further contact between Lucah and the family, even though Asina pleads for his sake, but it isn't to be.

The night before Lucah leaves, Asina beseeches her Goddess Mary to shield him. He sits with the family in the candlelight, saying the Lord's Prayer, when a profound energy lifts Lucah from his present conscious state. Asina sees he is encircled by luminous souls who capture his soul's consciousness. She watches as Jesus reveals Himself as a protector of Lucah's soul forever. The family reverberate within the heavenly energy that has filled the room. Lucah falls into a deep sleep after prayers as if in a trance.

He doesn't understand the conditions of his leaving, even though they've been explained to him. The torment of loss and grief in the night overcomes Lucah and Asina. She feels as though she's abandoning Lucah. She believes he'll think that she's giving him away by handing him over to them. She wants his family to take responsibility for taking him and for him to feel that they're the ones responsible for him not seeing Asina and the family again.

Morning arrives and they're up having breakfast when a car horn sounds in front of the house. There's no knock on the door. Nettie calls out, "They've arrived early for Lucah." Panic sets in Lucah as he looks at Asina.

Asina wants to run. She says to Lucah, "I can't give you away, Lucah."

Nettie opens the door. Lucah stands on the top step, frozen. No one moves in the car to come and get him. He looks around for Asina, who's shaking uncontrollably inside the house. Asina is stunned and silent. Her thoughts are clouded. Asina unknowingly is reliving the past of losing Ralia in her body without her mind's awareness.

Something breaks inside her. She walks to the door as Lucah walks to her. They hug and hold each other. Neither wants to be the first to let go.

The horn again blasts loudly. Lucah startles in Asina's arms. He turns and walks outside, carrying his few favourite belongings. He moves quickly to the open gate and turns to Asina, who is standing on the front step. They don't wave to each other. His face is ashen. He's gone. Asina doesn't know what he's thinking or how he'll process the loss.

The grieving and the yearning for Lucah in the family is insurmountable. Asina constantly feels Lucah fretting for her, and she feels pain in her chest from the tremendous loss he must be feeling. Asina is unaware that she has become her mother's shadow.

Asina describes the feeling to Sentel and her children. "It feels like Lucah has died, but we can't close the lid of the coffin, and there's no funeral. Therefore, there can be no closure for us or for Lucah. This grieving will just go on."

Life just doesn't go back to the way it was for any member of the family.

Asina has no memory of the pain of Ralia leaving Ezara. In fact, Asina has little connection with her past or to her future. She only lives in the now, always feeling she's wanting to go home. She doesn't understand these feelings that rise and fall in her. To her, they seem to come at the most inopportune times. She can fall into depression with these feelings of displacement and abandonment that linger on in her life. Even being with Sentel and her children, she's not able to identify the feelings or to understand their meaning in her life.

The family are coming to gather to celebrate Lucah's birthday as they have celebrated each year since he left them. The phone call comes at work telling Sentel that Lucah has taken his life the night before. Sentel is immediately broken. All he can think is, "I can't tell Asina." He panics and calls to tell Nettie and to ask her to come with him to tell her mother. He says to her, "I must tell her. I must be there for her." She comes immediately to accompany him and they both slowly try to process the news while driving.

Asina is at work in her office when they find her. She knows there's something wrong when they both arrive together, as they both should be at their own work. She turns and walks away from them, feeling their enormous energy that something is wrong.

Asina falls to the ground, screaming, "No. No. Not Lucah. How do I live with that for the rest of my life? How will I ever get that image out of my head?"

With that statement, she hears Lucah yell at her, "No, Mumma, not you! Not you, Mumma!"

Guilt, remorse, anger, and the futility of living on without him and needing to run away are only some of the first reactions that deluge Asina's mind. All she can think of to say to Sentel and Nettie is, "Lucah chose not to stay. He has decided to take himself home to the arms of Jesus. I knew he wouldn't cope. They didn't listen to me. Now we all are to live with his choice."

Hearts are smashed, and bodies are limp. Asina hugs Nettie and Sentel and softly sobs. She stays a long time in their embrace. They comfort each other, realising Lucah is no longer here. Asina doesn't comprehend. His photo remains in her hands.

In the night, Asina feels Lucah lying beside her bed on the little mattress he always dragged in just to be with her when he woke sick or frightened.

The funeral brings the two families together. There are apologises for taking him and causing him suffering. Asina wails on the shoulder of the one she loved, cared for, and supported. There is only tragedy for both families.

Asina remembers that, during the years apart, the family saw Lucah only the few times when he would come himself to see them without telling her. Asina remembers him coming one day, having run away, wanting some of his personal belongings he left behind. He stayed for nearly an hour in his bedroom looking through photos, games and his baby toys. He left them in his box as he left.

The last time he ran away, he stayed a whole year with Asina. He phoned and told his family he wasn't coming back. They didn't try to get him back, and his stay ended when he delved into buying and selling drugs with and for his mates. He was caught and sent to a youth shelter. He continued his downhill behaviour until he died.

Asina's travels to the years ahead to where she sits alone, pondering the deaths of her mother, her son, and her daughter. Her grief is suppressed as it's too much for her to comprehend and process. Her unresolved grieving accumulates further and further and leaves her in a chronic state of survival. Sadness and grief accompany each family member throughout those coming years as they continue to live on.

PART 4

Loss

7

⟡Support

IN PRAYER, A LARGE, INVISIBLE BROWN cloak wraps around Asina's shoulders as she sits in torment. She feels Saint Francis in her immediate presence. She intuits from him the notion of living simply through her grief, as he lived. He tells her through his spirit, "Meet each day and each moment in the same spirit as that of a child. Look for simplicity in yourself and in your children and live there without the expectations of the world. Live in the present moment to understand."

He pulls back, leaving the impression in her to traverse from earthly wants into the world of spirit where she will find answers to her needs for surviving.

"Thank you for caring for me and for my children," Asina sighs gratefully.

The transition is easy for Asina. She dozes off to sleep in the presence of Jesus. His caress is as gentle as His words to her, "I'm every child you have ever loved." He soothes her as she lies curled up in the foetal position on her bed. She rests in peace wrapped in his love and his mesmerising presence.

As time escapes, Asina feels inadequate as a mother, and her thoughts go to her choice to marry instead of entering the convent. She doubts herself and pleads for clarity.

She cries out to her heavenly Mother, "Mother Mary, I'm a mother, and I'll do anything for my children and others' children. Everything has become too hard. I don't understand. I'm not coping. You're a mother, and you know what it's like when you can't help your child. Please help me, Mother! I beg you to do something to let me know you are there to help me forever."

Early in the morning, Asina startles awake to a car horn blasting out thunderous waves of sound just as the sun peeps over the horizon. She runs to the table to fetch the car keys just as Sentel grabs them. He runs downstairs to open the car door, thinking that opening it will stop the horn. It doesn't. He then opens the bonnet of the car to dislodge the wires connecting the horn, and as he is about to do so, the horn stops.

Asina stands on the top step, watching. Sentel turns to her with confusion and amazement on his face. "It just stopped by itself," he tells Asina. They stand there dumbfounded as to what caused the horn to go off. He comes upstairs, and they try to make sense of the event.

Sentel turns the kettle on for a morning cup of tea, and Asina puts two slices of bread into the pop-up toaster and presses them down to cook and goes to walk away to get the butter and honey. She notices that the toast slowly rises and then slowly goes back down again of its own accord. This occurs twice without her touching it. The two of them look in confusion at each other again.

"Something is happening!" Asina remarks. "This isn't normal."

Sentel agrees with her.

Asina feels alert and hyper-aroused and continues, "There's a large energy around us today. I need to contact the kids. I feel Mary is coming today."

Asina phones all her children and tells them, "Mary is coming. Be ready for her messages."

The children know their mother very well and acknowledge her announcement. They have seen their mother in her spiritual consciousness many times.

Asina listens to the signs of the day and goes out into her large front garden and sets a garden chair near the once-working waterfall amongst the overhanging trees. There's only green foliage in the garden and one old, small rose bush with three roses on it on the distant side of the garden far from the area she has chosen.

By 2:30 p.m., Asina sits down with her rosary beads and begins to pray the rosary that Ezara taught her as a child. Her daughter Neena and her sister Nica arrive by 3:00 p.m., and more chairs are sought. They continue saying the rosary together.

Clouds begin to form in the clear blue sky. Gushes of wind bring in the clouds. One cloud lowers and hovers over the small tree in front of them on the top tier of the garden. The wind stops, and every leaf on the tree stops trembling. It's so eerily silent and still that the three women hush their prayers and their talking and listen to the silence.

Asina stares into the sky above the small tree. Her eyes become transfixed. She describes what she's seeing to the others. "There are magnificent colours swirling around in an orbit. A woman, I think it's Mary, is appearing inside the orbit, and she has a small globe of light in her hands. A child is appearing within this globe. I think it's her child, Jesus."

Asina holds her gaze fixed and watches intently for what seems a long time to the others who aren't seeing anything but are feeling a very different energy than previously.

Asina tell the others, "The child looks like two-year old Lucah, and he's sitting on her lap. He's reaching out to us. There's a tall man standing to the back of Mary, and he's smiling at us."

The vision continues, and Asina doesn't take her eyes away from the unfolding phenomenon. She listens intently for a message, but there are no words. Asina tries to explain what she's intuiting.

She tells the others, "I asked for help, and He has sent His Mother, the beautiful lady in the light, to us in my garden, and she shows me that she has two-year old Lucah sitting on her lap. She is Lucah's Mother and protects him in her loving arms. She is letting us all know that she's supporting us and she's supporting our children."

Asina eventually looks at the others as the light fades into the sun. Mother Mary disappears, leaving an overpowering perfume of roses for the women, as strong as if it was just sprayed on after a hot shower.

Neena goes to find the outdoor statue of Mary that her mother has standing at her front door. She carries it in her arms and places it in the very position Asina tells her where Mother Mary was standing in the vision. The women tidy the area and go to pick the three roses off the bush nearby – one for each of them, a gift they take home and place beside their beds in remembrance.

Asina is overwhelmed with joy when Sentel comes home from work. Even though he has missed Mary's appearance as he had to work, he believes his wife. The following days are peaceful, and Asina feels a sense of great calm and that she can now manage.

Each day, she visits the place of the vision, her sanctuary, and sits and prays the rosary by herself. She places flowers in the place where Mary appeared, feeling Mary's presence there each day as the cloud comes on the wind and stops above the small tree. The wind stops, and although she doesn't see Mary, she knows she's there with her.

The adult children are leaving for a trip to the city when Asina is sitting in the sanctuary saying her rosary. She waves them goodbye and continues to move her hands along the beads, saying the Hail Marys.

She comes to the end of the rosary. Her index finger and thumb of her right hand are on the chain at the end of the last decade, and her index finger and thumb on her left hand are on the chain before the first Lord's Prayer at the beginning of the rosary.

As she says the last prayer, "Glory be to the Father and to the Son and to the Holy Spirit," and finishes the rosary, she looks down at her fingers. She sees the chain between her fingers on both hands have turned to gold. Gold chain links have appeared on Asina's rosary beads where there previously was silver chain in her hand.

She gasps and tears well up in her eyes. She murmurs, "She's telling me He's the beginning and the end." His Mother has left an indelible sign on her beads to remind her each day as she prays her rosary that she's supported and loved forever. Asina holds the beads to her heart and allows the energy from the beads that now have the deep fragrance of roses to heal her broken heart. She's healed. She accepts that she and her family are blessed.

Asina learns the power of the rosary beads when they hold the perfume indicating Mary's presence. She uses the beads when they emit the rose fragrance to intuit her messages as Mary guides her to do so. Asina and her family practice simplicity and become present in the here and now. As the family is taken further into finding their souls, their approach eases tensions and opens the way for understanding and patience to grow and flourish.

She realises that Nettie's child, her grandchild, arrives on earth just before Mary's arrival, and it's shortly afterwards that Nettie wanders into Ezara's old neighbourhood to buy a business without Asina's knowledge. She tells her mother of her purchase after the settlement.

Asina is pleased Nettie has made the decision to further herself, but she tells her daughter, "Nettie, that's where I grew up. I haven't been there since my mother Ezara passed. In fact, the business you've bought was frequented by my mother."

Nettie is surprised. "You've never told me of this place before. Mum. I didn't know this about you. Come and see it, please."

"That means I'll need to touch my memories. I don't think I can, Nettie," Asina sighs.

"You're so much a part of this venture, Mum. This isn't a coincidence that I've walked into your life so profoundly. You need to come and open to your soul," Nettie pleads.

Asina begins to remember. "I haven't opened my soul to feel my mother for so many years. She told me I would forget her. She was right. I can't believe I moved on without her. It was crushing for me when she left."

Now the fears of opening that part of her is upsetting to Asina. As she's driving home to Nettie's home, they pass the hospital where Ezara died. Asina has passed this way many times before, but this time a scream inside of Asina wants to come out as she remembers leaving Ezara in the hospital just after she passed. Her memory takes her to that place inside herself where she left Ezara behind.

The scream of pain is still inside Asina. No grieving has been done. She suppressed the pain almost thirty-five years ago. Now it's surfacing. Nettie's baby sits in the back seat of the car, watching Asina begin to grieve for the first time.

Asina decides that she'll visit Nettie's shop with her. She stays with Nettie overnight and opens her heart up to her daughter about her beloved Ezara and her life with her mother.

Asina begins to feel her mother's presence. She feels her loving hands touching her, and she hears her voice whispering to her for the first time. Asina asks Nettie, "How have I been able to block her out for so long?" Nettie holds her mother's hand and doesn't know what to say to her.

8

Reunion

ASINA GOES ON A JOURNEY IN her dream state. She goes to look for Ezara alive in the little house. She sees her sick in bed, just as she was on that last day before she went to hospital. Asina can't see her face, but she can see she's wearing the same nightgown that she was wearing in hospital. Asina wonders why she hasn't been to see her mother. She feels shock and guilt and apologises to her mother for not visiting her for so long. She can't understand why she would do such a hurtful thing to Ezara. She begins to worry that something is wrong.

Still in the dream, she sees Ezara get up and walk to her wardrobe in her bedroom with her back to Asina. She tries again to talk to her mother, but she doesn't turn around. All she hears her mother say to her is, "Everything has changed."

Asina is left confused and wakens from her dream, feeling great sorrow. Lying in her bed on her own, she realises Ezara is gone. Her heart and soul wrench open, and for the first time, she has allowed herself to feel the reality of her loss.

Asina tells Netttie, "I have to walk the streets where we once walked. I need to see the house that we lived in. I want to visit the marketplace, to see the old school, and go into the church Ezara took us to."

Nettie offers to take her back to the area where she once lived. "We'll go there for you just to look around."

Asina is excited and yet nervous as she and Nettie and the baby drive to Ezara's little house. Nettie pulls up in front of the house, and they both stare at the quaint little dwelling. They get out and walk up to the front gate. Asina feels the familiarity of the fence and the gate by rubbing her hands over the old iron structure. Asina remarks, "Not much has changed. The gardens are nicely kept as Ezara would have them, and the fruit trees are bearing. The old fallen log, my horse, has been removed, and a shed has been built there."

They see that the house is occupied. They walk past and notice

Larone's house next door is for sale and is empty. They decide to wander into her yard and walk up the stairs to look through the windows. They find the front door ajar, so they call out to see if anyone is there. There's no answer. They step into the front room and realise the house is completely empty. They look at each other, and their thoughts collide. At once both dare to go in further and take a quick look around. Asina feels the intense energy and sees where she played as a child. She gasps for breath. Just as quickly, they leave and pull the door shut and escape to the car. Asina is speechless.

Quickly, they drive off as if leaving a scene of a crime and drive through the township. They pass the many homes and shops she remembers and the school she attended. It's as if she's stepped back in time. Asina asks to keep going on further to the church hoping they can catch Mass this Sunday morning feeling as if they need absolution for what they had done.

They enter the church just as the service starts. Asina takes them to the same pew that Ezara always sat in with her all those years ago. Asina is flooded with memories. The angels are still looking at her, and the sun still shines on the painting, making it come alive. The light fittings are the same, and the alcove at the back of the church contains the same life-size statue of Mary.

After the service and people have left the church, they walk slowly to the back alcove to absorb its surrounds. Slowly, they leave through the old wooden doors and onto the paved porch with paved steps flowing down onto the footpath.

As Asina steps down the first few steps, she excitedly tells Nettie, "I can feel Ezara's arm through mine as she always did for support, and I can hear her little high-heel shoes clicking beside me on the steps as I walk down each step. I just want to stay here with her. I just want to be with her!"

Instead of going back to the car, they choose to walk to the little marketplace near the river. Asina walks through the market stalls and smells all the familiar, fresh food products again. She buys fresh fruit and little cakes to eat for their stroll through Asina's memories. They wander to the banks of the river where she played. They sit on the grass to eat, and Asina's mind meanders back to old times that she spent here with Ezara and Ralia.

She's lost in recall when she notices Nettie. "Are you all right?" she asks her daughter. Asina sees that she has dark rings under her eyes and is very pale.

Prior to this time, Nettie hasn't shared many details of her life with Asina as any matter of urgency, but since Nettie stumbled alone into Asina's life, unscheduled moments like these are happening more often, filled with deep insights between Nettie and her mother.

Nettie decides to fully confide in her mother. "Mum, my relationship isn't working. I'm overwhelmed with our financial burdens of paying off the house and trying to make household bills and taking care of the children." She pauses. "I bought the business here as an investment whilst maintaining my career, thinking it would bring in that extra money." Nettie struggles finding the words. "But I'm doing all of this on my own. I'm raising the children on my own with no support." She stops and is now crying.

Asina hugs her daughter and waits for her to calm. She's very aware that things have not been going well for Nettie for a long time. They both sit limply on the grass, pondering the future. Asina looks at Nettie carrying a tired, little baby in her arms, and she sees that Nettie is not well and she's emotionally and physically exhausted from the years of the constant attempts to resolve her marital and financial problems.

Her thoughts return to Ezara. She feels she must leave her again after just finding her. Just by going home with Nettie, her thought creates instant pain, so excruciating and so familiar. She relives her leaving the only source of love, who was always Ezara. The heaviness enters her chest cavity, and her shoulders sink. As a child, she had to leave each Sunday after another interchange between her two homes was over.

She gathers herself. She looks at the baby in his mother's arms and knows that from this moment she's with her own mother Ezara forever on a mystical journey. She feels her soul rapidly fill up with warmth and love like gushing rainwater pouring off the roof, overflowing the gutters, racing through the down pipes, and thundering into the spout uncontrollably flooding the reservoir while trying to fill an empty tank with fresh drinking water after a long drought. Like the tank, she's filled to the brim and overflowing with her mother's love. She's at peace.

Asina stays another night with Nettie as she's on her own with the children. They talk further about Nettie's plight. "It's really bizarre, Mum. I don't even know why I've taken on this business. I don't understand why I'd embark on an adventure that's so obscure to my life. It's so unsettling how much this area involves your life, though. It's like I've walked right into your world and I didn't even know I was doing it. Still, it's like I'm meant to be here. Every time I drive here, I get this overwhelming feeling that I just don't understand why I'm here. Why, Mum? What's happening?"

"I really don't know, but I sense that Ezara is calling us to respond to your needs, Nettie, and to my need to find her through you," Asina haltingly replies.

"I know, Mum, but you are involved in my life at this time for some other significant reason," Nettie replies, accepting the fact that Asina's participation was also going to be needed during a difficult separation.

"Well, I know that I've got to come back to walk the streets with Ezara, Nettie. I feel so emotionally drawn back here," Asina desperately tells her.

With this conversation at the forefront of her thoughts, Nettie accepts the synchronicity that her new business is in the heart of Asina's childhood. She has intuitively been guided towards something far more profound than she could ever imagine. Nettie intuitively knows that her life, as well as Asina's, is about to change.

Asina's contact with Ezara after all these years finally opens her silenced heart and soul to hear and feel her mother who has willingly come to be with her. *But what is she trying to tell me?* Asina wonders.

A strange sensation encapsulates her whole being. She whispers to Nettie, "I feel that we have managed to stumble into an unknown reason that surrounds the connection between both of us and Ezara. I also sense that we have also tripped into our own personal unfolding stories here. Our inner yearnings to discover our own selves has led us to where we are yet to uncover the secrets of the interconnecting generations."

Nettie gasps and nods in agreement.

Asina's relationship with Nettie blossoms as Nettie discloses many aspects of her life to her mother. Asina comes to understand that Nettie's growth as an individual continues to be sabotaged. She knows of this effect in her own relationship. Nettie is unravelling many sore points in her that she hasn't successfully handled in herself.

In time, they become support for each other and spend many hours together, discussing aspects of relationships. They shuffle Nettie's children between them so she can attend to her business. In fact, Asina feels she's reliving her own life with her children in their business.

Soon, the strain on Nettie trying to juggle her children, home, and work and Asina running her own family business and career is visibly showing on both women.

"Well, what do we do at this point?" Asina asks Nettie. "We're trying to carry the full load without any care or support for us."

She continues, "Just imagine it. You're a pack horse carrying an enormous load up a hill, and you're nearly at the top, but you physically cannot go any further. Your master begins to beat you to make you obey his commands. Of course, he believes that he has every right to beat you.

"Now if you're capable of physically moving, the beating will be effective, and you'll eventually move because of the pain. However, if you're physically incapable of moving, you cannot move however hard you are beaten. In fact, each whipping will continue to deplete any remaining capability of movement within you. I see you like the horse, Nettie."

Asina stops for a breath and watches her daughter's eyes as she intensely processes the analogy. Asina continues her story.

"Having become a subservient companion and having survived many hardships over such a long life together, you desperately want to please your master, but you cannot overcome your physical limitations. You collapse and your master is left screaming angrily at you and bitterly thrashes you and demands you to get up immediately and to continue to carry the load."

Asina sighs heavily, knowing full well the weight of such a load and the incapacity of carrying it any further. "The horse will give up eventually beaten and broken, and it will lose its will to live," Asina firmly states.

"Will you become broken and give up and die, Nettie?" Tears well up in Nettie's eyes.

Asina is also realising that she's expressing her own feelings too.

Nettie also knows that her mother has been that horse so many times and she and her older siblings have helped their mother get to the top of the hill.

But today, the tears fall down Nettie's cheeks and roll over her flushed face as she comes to the undeniable truth that she's the horse. Her own health has slowly deteriorated so that she's incapable of moving any further. For Nettie every possible option to share the load has been considered and implemented, and now with a business, no money left, no resources, and more importantly, failing health, all attempts of getting up and making life better is near impossible. The need for the release from the shackles that bind her to her load is paramount.

Acceptance slowly penetrates as they sit and peer into each other's eyes. "Trying to pick up more of the load is no longer an option," Asina states emphatically. "If you do it the same way again, you'll be undone again." They search each other's faces for that significant impetus for change—the how.

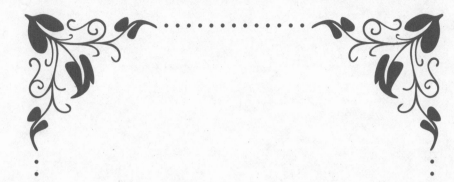

Part 5

Survival

9

Mystery

As their sacred journey opens, Nettie and Asina become very aware that they're being directed by a perceptive and very insistent power that overshadows their own thoughts. They awaken each day within their surreal stage play where each character or event they encounter enters at the right moment. This miraculous feeling is the most exhilarating of all. These unknown happenings begin to mystically capture their reliance on God's power. They both believe that this is the way to live forever, where all is predetermined and there's no fear in not knowing what's to happen next.

Although it's unnerving, each moment unfolds yet another piece of their puzzle. No matter how hard they try to control the events, they have a life of their own. They believe they have entered a bubble floating out in space where all events and characters collide with perfect balance and poise in exact formation required to exist in perfect harmony within the universe. They know they're protected and loved and mysteriously guided to keep walking and to keep discovering the mystery of life, their lives.

Both women make the promise to each other that they'll find the "how" this time around the circle. Nettie begins, "We'll set out to do the impossible, whatever that is, at all costs, and no matter what happens, we'll support each other with the intention that we'll find another way to exist. We promise each other that no one will get left behind and we will walk with each other to the end of the journey towards our own independence." They hold hands and promise.

With their intention very clear, they acknowledge Nettie's next statement. "With the love that resides deep within us for each other, we'll remain present and aware as a state of being, for each other and for ourselves, as we walk our own individual journeys of change side by side until their end. We acknowledge that as love cannot be lost, it therefore can never leave us."

Asina responds, reassuring Nettie, "Yes. For us to become our souls, we'll pass through each step necessary to reach our soul's goal." At this stage, neither of the women know of their future lives to come.

Asina continues, "We'll stay in this state of reliance on God's love, and we'll no longer be taken over by our own constant thoughts of worthlessness. We will believe that we really are spiritual beings walking with God, and we'll not let our negative thoughts overcome us. We will believe that we really can be in God's stillness and have the freedom to be enlightened and to enlighten, and to be loved and to love."

Nettie listens intently to her mother. "From now on, we'll strive to become our souls by traversing negativity and taking steps to honour ourselves. We will be our souls' guardians. We will protect them from our repetitive negative patterns that keep us victims. We will become our souls."

Asina ponders as she speaks. "Becoming our souls will keep us in God's silence, and then our thoughts will be loving and tender, and we'll find hope, and we'll become peace. Outer peace will no longer be the option – our peace will only come from within."

"You know, Nettie," Asina continues, "Mary sent an indelible sign that she's with us. She's opening our souls by sending Ezara to guide us. She's brought us to this place in time, and she'll walk with us as we become our souls."

"Peace is within each of us, isn't it, Mum?" Nettie asks her mother. "I now realise that I have been forever searching for external peace. You know, Mum, you're far closer to achieving that internal peace than I am. It's in detaching from external wants that all will be gained internally, and this will give us peace, not despair."

"Actually, Nettie, we're so close to this inner peace. We just have to help each other remain focused on our intentions."

Nettie continues to run the business, attend to the children, and hold on to her career with study while her relationship continues to deteriorate until it becomes impossible for her to remain any longer.

Following her deepest intuition, Nettie leaves one night after another disagreement and flees with her children to come directly to her mother's home.

Asina knows that Nettie and her children are almost physically depleted when they arrive at her home after having endured the argument and experienced the extreme fear of leaving.

When the children are in their beds, Asina and Nettie lie on the bed in the guest house with an awful heaviness in their stomachs and a tight restriction in their chests stopping inhalations of full breaths.

The practicalities of how Nettie will continue her career, keep the business going, manage the children's needs and their education, collect their belongings, and settle into a new life are forceful thoughts that spin round in their heads.

The following months prove to become the most dramatic change to each of their lives. The year ensues slowly amid the chaos of a new school, sorting out access, finding new resolutions to the same arguments, and managing the children's emotions almost moment by moment.

Nettie reminds her mother, "We're well and truly on our spiritual journey together now, and we need to use the new strategies. You know, Mum, your life has closely echoed mine. If we don't replicate our old behaviours, the consequences will also not be replicated."

During this time, Asina is trying to keep her business going and managing another established business with Nettie's father, including a second store he pressured her to open. Asina is angry with herself that she has given in to his demands again. She is so accustomed to his old ways of dominancy to get what he wants.

Nettie tersely tells her mother, "We somehow think that we're the only people who can fix these situations that are created for us to live in. But this isn't the truth. They just don't want to do what we do, and they sure as hell won't do shit all if we're going to keep picking up the entire load. They're playing us like fools, Mum. No wonder we're screaming. Stuff this. Let them figure it out themselves."

Asina hears her daughter's inner scream that has finally become an outward expression.

"The question is, will we really do everything that it will take to be finally free of this chaos from our lives?" Nettie questions. "Or will we wait till our last breath? It's exactly that, our last breath!" Nettie stares at her mother.

"I'm not doing it your way, Mum. Not for anyone. I just want to live.

I want to play with my kids and to take one full breath of fresh air and laugh and smile!" Nettie asserts.

Yet something in her body knows that these words are only a dream to hold onto for now. "Reality means losing everything. I'm losing everything right now, Mum."

"I'm too old, Nettie. That's not what I want. Your father and I came back together after years apart, and we're trying to put things right. Yes, he still uses his old ways of getting what he wants and puts me in the middle of him achieving the results. But now that the economy is faltering, I need to give up my career and go back into running one store and he the other just to hold on to what we've regained. I know what I don't want. I don't want to lose it all again!" Asina states anxiously.

"But you just get beaten and beaten because they get angry in themselves and want more and more!" Nettie screams.

Holding on to the only piece of self-respect remaining in her soul of gentle kindness and sensitive spirit, Asina's hands cup her fallen face as Nettie speaks. Unknown to Nettie, another dispute transpired that morning between Asina and Sentel that left her body without energy. Now as she lies on the bed with her arm flung helplessly over her dark eyes in despair, she too fights internally for the motivation to keep going differently.

The air is filled with a heavy energy as Asina rises from the bed and goes to the kitchen. As she cracks each egg into the bowl, she remembers sitting with Ezara as she also made delicious delicacies as an act of soothing the soul. Nettie follows her to the kitchen. "How do you go from such despair to making pancakes, Mum?" she asks her mother in bewilderment.

"It soothes my soul. Ezara always did this, and now I know the truth behind why," Asina softly replies. She can feel her face regain its colour, and life is a possibility for her.

"Let's create what they could have become," Nettie suggests.

"Do you mean Ezara and Larone?" Asina had told Nettie the story of her neighbours when she lived with Ezara as a child.

"Yes, I do," she replies excitedly as if she knows a mystery is about to unfold.

Asina poses the questions to Nettie while she tentatively sips her hot cup of tea and eats one of the freshly made pancakes and licks the honey dripping down her hand. "Okay then, did they make the choice to stay in their relationships or to leave? Did they find the answers they were looking for? Did they find their freedom in their relationships? Did they achieve their fullness of their own life? If given a chance to just to be themselves who would they have been? Did they become their souls? Just who was Larone and who was my Ezara?"

Asina discloses to Nettie, "I guess when you're the only one sitting at your mother's side as she lay dying, wiping her tears, stroking her legs, and soothing her fears, I knew her then, and I know her now."

Asina ponders seriously, "I know Ezara to be a very meticulous person with a strong mind and will and with an eye for beauty, and I've tried to live up to her independence and strong will."

She continues, "I came into Ezara's life when she was around my age now, and I found her to be very passionate for life. She was very creative in her sewing and cooking. She was a pastry cook early in her life with her husband who was a baker. They ran their own store. She was very caring for those in need, and this was shown through her care for me, for Ralia, and for Siroda. She was very caring for her sister and her children in their time of need, and she was a good friend, especially to Larone through her troubles.

"I see her as a pure young girl from the warm Atlantic islands with sallow skin and a sparkle in her dark eyes and a passion for life. She needed a passionate love and a fullness of life for honouring her uniqueness. Instead, she married a staunch man from war-torn Europe with five brothers, who took her purity to himself before marrying her. In her time, that was a family stigma for a young woman to live with.

"I wasn't told much about their relationship issues. I was left to decipher it without the details as I grew older. When I knew him, he was an alcoholic and left her on her own most of the time while he went away for days, weeks, and months.

"Secrets were very prevalent in families then. From the pieces I do have, she arrived on her own with Siroda to the area you wandered into to create a new life without him. Separation was not mentioned, only lived out, and divorce was out of the question with both their families being Catholic."

10

Women

NETTIE EXPLAINS INTUITIVELY, "WE MUST HONOUR these two women and understand what is now being filtered from them to us from their spirit side. This is a very spiritual experience and we must recognise it for being so."

Nettie continues, "Mum! They needed to find things that were beneficial to their lives, just as you did with your career. They needed to concentrate on their strengths, their passion for life, their uniqueness, and their own personal development so that they could give of their true selves. Did they do this, Mum? Let's uncover their lives together as we uncover ours."

"Nettie, you're strong, independent, and passionate, prepared to take risks, and not afraid of being in the world on your own. You've taken your children on your own and ready to etch out a new life for them and yourself. I'm still sitting silent, but fiercely independent," Asina solemnly assesses.

She falls silent and becomes absorbed in her thoughts. She's dazed by the recollections coming to her like waves crashing onto a rocky shore.

"Mum! Hello! Where are you? You have gone into one of your places again!"

Nettie intrudes into Asina's daze. Asina responds as she slowly attempts to assimilate reality and the effect of the past that is regenerating through her whole being. She's beckoning Lucah into her thoughts again.

"Oh, Nettie, I have already replicated Ezara's life with Lucah. We had him for many years before he was taken back. As was Ralia taken back. I know the pain of the grief of his leaving. I have walked her footsteps until now." Asina feels the pain all over again.

"If I look closer at the similarities in my life and Ezara's life, I see that she ran a business too. But I also became formally educated in my adult life. She didn't have a chance to do that, although she was educated through the experiences she lived as I have been and continue to be.

Nettie, you also have been educated formally and continue to study as you raise your children."

"Tell me about Ralia, please, Mum," Nettie pleads.

"She was a baby when she was given to Ezara by her parents. Ezara mothered her until Ralia was eleven years old, then her parents took her back. Siroda was not married then and still lived at home with Ezara. The parents lived in the room upstairs. Having become very familiar with each other during their stay, they decided to leave her with Ezara, saying they would be back after a short holiday. In fact, her father was due to go off to war, and her mother didn't want to be on her own raising a child. Her father eventually visited when he came back as a wounded soldier, years after leaving her. They asked Ezara to bring her to them."

Asina takes a deep breath with tears in her eyes as she remembers what really happened all those years ago, not her child's version.

"Oh my God!" Nettie blurts out and put her hand over her mouth gasping. "Ezara lived through you after Ralia left. It was through you that she expressed her pain and her passion for life. This is the reason why her own daughter didn't know her, but you did. She filled you with the confidence and love and demanded a better life for you than she had for herself or Siroda."

Asina listens to Nettie's words and realises that she speaks the truth. She replies, "A heavy responsibility always lay in my heart to fulfil my dreams for Ezara. She was always a reason why I didn't enter the convent. I couldn't leave her."

"How old were you when your grandfather died?" Nettie enquired.

"It was sometime after Ralia was taken back. Ezara would have had two deaths to cope with around the same time! I remember the sombreness in the air around her, and I felt the great sorrow, although I really didn't know what was happening. Ezara became finally free to fly from the cage that entrapped her all those years when he died, but did she fly?" Asina thinks out loud. "Maybe not."

"I have vivid memories of him just turning up any time, staying a few days, and then leaving again. I felt the pain in Ezara's eyes when he came and when he left. I remember only one Christmas that he came home. It was the year I went to live with Siroda. She knew him very well and was guarded with him. She didn't seek him out purposely. I walked up the hill from the house and waited for him to get off the bus, and I held his hand as we walked together to the house."

Nettie sits and ponders the story. She closes her eyes, lays her head back on the chair, and quietly says, "I'm so tired that I can't even hold my posture upright."

Nettie confirms, "I have an inner tiredness not to be compared with weariness but more an inner exhaustion that has penetrated every cell of my body, where my body aches from within and my mind is clouded, and my thoughts confused. My bare basic functioning has even slowed." Nettie stops and her mind wanders.

"The concept of responding to my child is insurmountable, and the idea of a normal day is beyond all my capabilities. My mind is attuned to just surviving for one day, with my focus toward the moment where the day ends, and I can finally rest. Even then, I know that my mind won't rest and the battle between the mind and my body will last for hours into the night until I pass out at some point, only to wake to another day of the same, if not worsened, deterioration within moments of awakening. My body hasn't even left the bed, yet it aches," Nettie finishes.

Asina responds to Nettie, knowing her daughter is not well and has undertaken too much. "Only a woman tired from carrying the whole load herself could feel like this. I always thought it was just me feeling so tired that life passes by in a blur," Asina states as she now envisages Larone sweeping the cement as she played on the swing beside her. "Larone told me all of what you just explained to me in that one interaction many years ago."

"Tell me, Mum, why Larone was so tired. I know the many children would have been a lot for her to carry," Nettie comments.

Asina replies, "Silence within families and close friends was taught stringently and by hard lessons in the past. Ezara and Larone had so much in common that they became great allies and each other's confidants in their joys and sorrows. The two women were soul mates. They knew more of each other than they ever said to anyone. They understood and accepted the plight of women in those days. I feel their intense presence as we uncover how women lived in silence and kept their secrets. No wonder they came back together now to heal the next generations.

"As soon as I entered that house that day, I felt the presence of something dark, and there was a spirit that obviously didn't want me there. I believe that I was there intuitively knowing there was a secret attached to the house so the house could be healed by my mere presence pressuring the spirit of darkness to leave. This I believe with all my heart."

Asina recoils into herself as if some great curative energy left her soul and had found a place to heal and rest inside that house.

"What are you saying, Mum?" Nettie demands.

She tells Nettie, "We'll never know, but we can only imagine a very old and sinister secret." Asina has nothing more to say as she feels great relief from such secrets that she unknowingly has retained since she was a child.

Nettie announces with a certain amount of freedom in her voice, "Mum, finally I'm left alone to do what means the most to me. The fact that I'm not the one who's finishing off our affairs, that I'm here fulfilling the kids, is why I bought the store in the first place. It's not possible for me to clean up and sell the house because interacting feels like having someone physically kick you in the stomach over and over until you are kneeled over protecting your vital organs." She explodes verbally while holding her stomach.

Nettie continues, "You know, Mum, I could lose my desire to be me for my children so easily, but the need to teach them to be themselves requires passion from me, and passion is not there without me being my full authentic self."

Nettie takes a deep breath and continues, "To be ripped of all that you are; to protect your children from any more emotional pain; to stand between the external world and your children as the only means of buffering them from the reality of the harshness of life is one thing. But to have a child's ability to see the world as it is now; and to see past the stress of provisions, shelter, and futures and only care about the immediate needs of laughter, treats, and love is all I desire."

Nettie concludes very succinctly putting her feelings into words. Pointing to the middle of her chest, she finishes, "It's like I have this deepest pain here. It feels so empty, and it's so painful."

"That is where you heart is," Asina replies solemnly, recognising that Nettie is suffering the very feeling that she has avoided for years whilst still in her relationship. "I know why you haven't taken the action of separating earlier. You knew the pain that would ensue, and it's the pain that you're now living. Your love is so deep, and so is your pain of losing."

Nettie takes a deep breath and continues, "Mum, I think we're meant to finish off the women's stories, by living our stories differently. They didn't have the opportunity to complete their stories any other way than they did. But we'll find a way which they only dreamed of, for all our lives.

"It's we who will free not only our own souls, but their souls as well. We're meant to fly not only for ourselves, but for them. I can feel it every time I drive towards the shop. I hear messages in my spirit that they are barracking for us as our guardian angels. They are protecting us and sending us little detours every time we falter or get lost during the journey."

As Nettie expresses her deepest intuitions in this momentary realisation, her tears dry up, and Asina and Nettie find the source of their answers to their questions that they have asked themselves for a long time.

Nettie responds, "The answer is to be found in what it is these women didn't do, not what they did. They may have spoken the truth to each other, but they didn't speak the truth from the rooftops. They spoke it within their own safe sanctuaries to each other and in the presence of a little child who grew into a woman who can now speak the truth."

PART 6

Believe

11

At All Costs

Nettie remains separated and manages to sell the house and her business. She moves to the country, to a city close to her parents, and buys a house for herself and the children. Over time, Nettie's attempt to share the financial load proves fruitless, but she won't sell their home. To keep her career and further study during school hours and to have time to be at home with her children, Nettie manages to gain a study grant and works part-time.

Asina can now make plans to pick up her career part-time and still manage the shops with Sentel to support Nettie and the children. Both women renew their promise to support and care for each other and to make sure that they remain focused on becoming their own souls.

During the next year, Nettie finds that she's unable to work and study as much as she wants due to her continuous ill health. Doctors don't seem to know why she's unwell for so long with fatigue, nausea, and virus-type symptoms.

On her way home from the doctors again, two years later, she tells her mother, "Mum, I've finally found out why I've been so sick and tired for so long. I've been told that I have stage one cervical cancer." Nettie shocks Asina with this diagnosis.

Picking up the children from school later, Nettie tells Asina, "I refuse to get this far and give in because I don't simply have the energy to get up. Yet, I have every reason to self-destruct at this moment. There're critical moments in life, and this is one of them. I either self-destruct now or not!"

Nettie's tears roll down her face while she slowly drives the car through the school gates. "I don't know what I do in this position." She continues, "I guess my view has been narrowed down to a one-centimetre-square picture. If I looked at the big picture, I would blow my brains out." Nettie stops, calms, and takes a deep breath.

She parks the car and pulls herself together. She turns to her mother.

"What I do now will determine the rest of my future. I need to have a very clear intention, and today my intention is to heal my body through a life of peace and happiness, and to force the emotions and the toxins out of every cell in my body. I'll get the medical treatment necessary, and I'll live my life making the most of every moment.

"I don't know what else to do but intentionally distract myself to feel good. I guess I'm defaulting to doing whatever feels good. To even consider thinking only negatively about myself is a slippery decision. I need to go to where I want to be, not where I am." Nettie ponders, and Asina listens closely to her daughter's self-analysis.

Nettie continues, "Living another day in chaos and in my own self-abuse is beyond me. Treating myself with kindness, care, and gentleness is the only option that doesn't lead to self-abuse.

"I'm not saying to bury myself in external non-realities. I'm saying for me to be present in every moment and feel good about experiencing that moment." Nettie looks at her mother and realises Asina has a worried frown.

"Mum, I'm present in the moment now. I suddenly feel the simplicity in life. The colour of the roses, for instance, will become my source of life. I'll absorb the simplest things, like spending time with you right now, and joy becomes the distraction from heaviness.

"It's like I'm renewed, and I begin to see life from a new perspective. I'll go back to the beginning and experience all the important small things that I've overlooked. I'll start again with them and see them in a healing form."

Her decision of acceptance, and her decision that the physical threat will not be exacerbated by emotional residue, takes sheer determination and willpower.

Nettie knows that in all situations the truth is always revealed, so she keeps her promises to herself.

Life becomes a series of celebrations and events built into everyday happenings.

She organises trips for her and the children. They go to the beach, concerts, sporting events, camping, parties, shopping trips. They try gardening, refurnishing their rooms, watching DVDs, eating ice cream. They have sleepovers with cousins, build cubby houses, have picnics on the lounge floor, arrange visits to Asina's and other family and friends. There is travelling, fishing, swimming, art, cooking, cleaning, first air flights, playing, playing, and more playing.

She continues to work hard and long to achieve as much as she can. She achieves high distinctions in her studies and completes the research component of her Ph.D. and presents it to her colleagues. She receives tremendous accolades from her mentors and colleagues. She just needs to write it.

She has been in the house five years, and some of the children are becoming teenagers. Nettie hasn't been very well and feels the two-year remission is over. She visits the doctor and collapses there. She's taken to the hospital, where more tests show the progression of the cancer and the need for further treatment.

Nettie is devastated.

She wants to stay in her home for as long as she can, so Asina supports her and gets her to treatment and cares for the children. Treatment seems to have worked, and Nettie goes away for an overseas trip for a few weeks to recuperate with her older sister, Neena. She comes home refreshed and continues her life. However, she's weaker than before and needs to take it slower.

Asina spends most of her time with the family now. Nettie's greatest emotional pain comes when she realises her illness is heightening tensions in everyone, when her loving, caring soul wants only compassion and care in her hours of need.

She takes the children away for their two-week school holiday break, and on her return, she's in so much pain, she's almost bedridden. Nettie collapses again, and there's no further treatment possible. Nettie is now terminal.

She chooses to move in with her parents, with her children. Asina houses them, but it's only a matter of weeks before Nettie goes to hospital for an extended stay. She comes home on a morphine drip and on a palliative care program.

She relaxes well, and the need to settle her affairs is ominous. Nettie is horrified by the judgement that she'll not need the money, and all assets are to be unevenly split. Nettie exclaims in despair, "I've been left in the gutter to die with nothing!"

Nettie is broken. Her home is sold, and she gives up her will to live. She returns to hospital for the last time. She leaves her body and goes with her soul to heaven.

Asina questions herself, "Was the cost too high?"

12

Existence

EARLY MORNING. THE OTHER FAMILY MEMBERS, including the young children, wait anxiously for the final call. The children have been sent to a school event at the previous request of Nettie, when she'd strongly indicated that she didn't want the children anxiously waiting at home for the call that she'd gone.

The call is now made to Nettie's eldest sister, Marni, who is caring for the children and is waiting at home. She leaves immediately to collect them. As soon as they see their aunt arrive before the event is over, they know instinctively that their mother is gone. The shock is immediate. Silence is heavy in the car as they drive home. Once inside, Marni tells them.

Nettie watches as each of her children find out that they no longer have her with them. She watches as their faces contort with great pain and great loss and confusion. Then she sees her father and other siblings' similar reactions.

The awareness of those left behind is not the same for Nettie. She feels their pain as love and compassion for them. There is no fear or panic arousing in her as she experiences the feeling of travelling.

Asina prepares Nettie's body with the nursing staff. She chooses a fresh set of clothing Nettie liked and combs her daughter's hair in the same style she always wore. She takes the hospital scissors and cuts, so delicately, threads of her hair for herself and for Nettie's children for when they get older. She folds these threads into separate tissues and puts them with Nettie's other belongings.

She now needs to pack Nettie's suitcase and get ready to leave Nettie in the room where she has been with her.

The moment soon comes when all is ready, and Asina is to leave her child. Never has she walked out and left her child. It's a difficult moment, and Asina doesn't know how to leave. Panic ricochets through her body.

She calls out to Nettie. She hears Nettie's voice reply, "Take me with you, Mum. Don't leave me here! I'll always be with you."

Asina replies to Nettie, "I brought you in here. I'll take you with me as I leave." Both women walk out of the room bonded together.

Neena, who has accompanied them throughout the endless days of Nettie's stay in the hospital, has been waiting in the visitors' lounge while Asina tended to Nettie's body. When she sees Asina, Neena tells her that she's just met and talked to the wife of the patient in the room next door to Nettie, who's also leaving life. Neena explains that he's the man who lives in the farming area near Asina and owned the dog that Nettie knocked and killed some years earlier.

Neena explains how she used the encounter with the wife to apologise on Nettie's behalf for killing his beloved dog. Neena explained how it has haunted Nettie all these years, as she didn't know who owned the dog, and she couldn't make amends.

Nettie's already tending to things she has left undone on the earth. She's watching this encounter between the wife and Neena. She's leaving with Asina. She's tending to the children and sending loving energy to them. She's following the news of her leaving as it ripples into the wider family and community.

She begins to realise that she's continuing, and that her full consciousness is still existing as she travels forward along the dark path, calling out, "I'm here! I'm here! Where are you, Jesus? I'm here!"

Nettie sees a dim light in the distance appear in the intense darkness. This light brings her comfort, as she sees within the light that a distant figure is appearing.

Eventually, Nettie sees the light being step through the light. The being reaches out as a gesture of beckoning and welcomes her into the resplendent light. At the same instant, she's with her mother's soul, still travelling towards the being.

Asina and Nettie come to two massive open gates. The gates have overreaching arches, and they look like an entrance to a huge and ancient school. Asina is familiar with this practice of standing outside the gates to usher souls to the other side.

Through these gates, they see that the path leads to an entrance of a long, wide-open rotunda, where many souls are gathering inside. The path then leads towards the entrance of a further chamber. Asina stops and explains to Nettie that she can go no further. "Only you must pass through these gates, Nettie," she tells her daughter.

Asina feels like she's dropping her daughter off to school for the last time, but this time, she won't come back to pick her up. Nettie must go through the gates without her beloved mother.

Saying goodbye seems so normal to them as they turn towards each other for their farewell. Nettie feels apprehensive to go and leave her mother. Asina feels the fierce rip in her own heart. Neither say goodbye. They just let go of each other and whisper, "See you later."

With a wave to her mother, Nettie enters through the gates into the essence of the luminary who offered her the welcoming greeting. Nettie meets, for the first time, her great-grandmother, who is welcoming her home. She is Ezara. With joyful greetings, the two immerse themselves into the space flooded with light within the now-closed chamber. Nettie is blinded by the light. An overwhelming gasp hurtles up in Nettie and tries to escape, but she stifles the sound. Her great-grandmother leads her to a group of people Nettie recognises.

Nettie is welcomed by those she's known who've already left earth, including her younger brother. She is ecstatic to also meet family members she'd only heard of while living on the earth, especially her great-grandmother. Joyful greetings from many souls she'd met on earth are infusing the magnificent surroundings of the grand entrance.

Asina arrives home with Neena. She has Nettie tightly wrapped in her soul. She stops outside to collect herself before she goes in to see the children. She goes to the trampoline in the backyard and climbs onto it and starts to bounce slowly to ease the stiff energy within her body. She hasn't cried. She is anxious at seeing the children.

She feels silly with the others watching from the house. It's not expected behaviour, especially for a grandmother, but still she bounces with a gamut of confused feelings swirling around inside her. She sees the world from a distorted perspective. Everything is moving and, at the same time, staying the same. The movement matches her feelings. Her head spins with many thoughts of what happens from here, but she's incapable of formulating any plan.

The adults come outside to see what's happening. They ask their mother what she's doing. "I need to feel my body," she replies. "I feel as though I've died." Everyone steps back and watches Asina move slowly on the trampoline.

The kids have already been told that their mother's gone and have come outside to watch. They don't understand what's happening. "What are you doing, Grandma?"

With no reply, they get on the trampoline one at a time with her, and, soon, the four become a chaotic rhythm. Asina soon drops to her knees due to the irregular movement. They follow and fall over her. The release of their pent-up energy comes out in squeals of delight, laughter, tears, and constant movement. In the movement, they feel the tremendous shift of energy in their world. Nothing is the same. They feel lost. Unattached. Floating. Unstable.

"Mum, catch them," Nettie calls to Asina, who is struggling with all her strength to reach a plan of action. Moving to the edge, Asina is ricocheted by the propulsion of energy. She lands with her feet on the ground.

Asina is exhausted from the continuous bounce and heads inside. The children follow her like lost souls.

Asina feels a sombre mood inside. Her older children are looking at her differently. Suddenly, she feels their projections onto her. Not only are the children motherless, she's the mother who's lost her child. She felt this same feeling from the nursing staff when leaving the hospital. She and the children felt so conspicuous, when they just wanted to melt into the background.

They find their way together through the first few days of Nettie leaving, but the feelings don't go away. They meet many people through the preparations for the funeral, and the feeling of wanting to hide is further enhanced. The funeral day culminates in fears, tears, and the strong urge to withdraw, but the need to walk through the pain together is mandatory.

The church is almost full of people who the children and Asina hardly know. Nettie has made so many friends and work colleagues. It's a tremendous gathering of relatives as well. Almost as overwhelming as the gathering Nettie is experiencing simultaneously. "On earth as it is in heaven." Asina hears Nettie's voice.

Asina knows that souls in heaven and those on earth both celebrate together as a magnificent soul such as Nettie's passes through to the spirit realm and arrives home. It's our connection, manifested. She feels the energy of spirit infusing those nearest to Nettie as the portal opens and her soul enters heaven. The grandmother and all her children are surrounded and blessed by this oozing, etheric energy seeping through from the other side. The blessing is a gift of spirit to help the family cope and survive their grief.

Asina feels as though they're all floating through the funeral. The older priest officiating at the Mass reminds the congregation, and Asina especially, that Nettie lived through silence, hope, suffering, loss, survival, belief, and heaven as Christ did. She, too, was unheard, misunderstood, not loved in return for her love, abandoned, forsaken, deprived of basic rights, betrayed, and denied. She came to believe in her soul and returns to become her soul in heaven.

Asina again squirms in her seat as she hears the truth from the lips of the priest. The priest's validation that Nettie lived a life through her soul and died to save her children is felt by those present. Asina believes that now the children will live through their own steps of silence, hope, suffering, loss, survival, belief, and heaven, as their mother did. Asina's wish for them is to live fully without any further familial angst.

The confusion of being alive without Nettie lays heavily in Asina's mind. While Nettie was alive, Asina set up her home for Nettie with the children. When very ill, Nettie was given an area by herself. The children had their own rooms away from Nettie and near Asina. Asina arranged a buzzer for Nettie to use when she needed Asina, day or night. It was only at the end that Asina stayed with Nettie constantly.

Now, only days after the funeral, Asina hears Nettie's buzzer. She's confused. Surprised and overwhelmed, she goes to the buzzer beside Nettie's empty bed. She interprets the strange call as an urgent call from Nettie.

Asina knows Nettie is still existing and listening to everything that's happening as she tries to make decisions for the children—schooling, financial matters, and the requirements of Nettie's will for Asina and Sentel to be legal guardians for the children.

Asina doesn't know if she's making up Nettie's presence. The need to have Nettie sitting beside her, helping Asina with all the decisions, is so prevalent in Asina's mind. She won't cry. She holds her emotions so that the children don't see her sad. She believes she needs to be strong, and if she believes she has Nettie near, she copes. As soon as she doubts Nettie's presence, Asina wavers and almost drowns in the practicalities and the enormous loss in her family.

The buzzer tells Asina that Nettie needs her. She stops everything and waits. She believes Nettie needs her urgently and is telling her something.

13

Battle

A S THE FAMILY PROCESSES THEIR LOSS on earth, so does Nettie process her arrival in heaven. The being of light Nettie now knows is her great-grandmother Ezara leads Nettie to many other luminaries she recognises, though she only had short periods of experience in life with them on earth.

There is the man whose dog she killed, who she'd had a chance to apologise to as they'd both crossed. She meets her friend from her youth who'd died so young. Nettie had been gutted by her death, and she'd felt her presence often after she'd passed. Nettie had loved her and now takes the opportunity to reconnect with her. She finds her as a beautiful being of light. She meets neighbours and acquaintances from work, school, and family she knew both long ago and very recently.

Others she knows well. Her two grandfathers and both grandmothers, aunts and uncles, and cousins, but most of all, her younger brother, Lucah, who hasn't left her side since her arrival. He showers her with an abundance of love. He shows her techniques of travelling in an instant to where she wants to go and how to navigate the new realm. They team up together to contact the family with the family pets they shared together on earth.

Their loving energy together already overwhelms the family, as the family have told Asina they've heard from both Nettie and Lucah.

Nettie is shown by Lucah that the realm she's in now is very much like the earthly realm, but it has more vivid colours and luminous vibrations of energy and light. She notices that there's no angst in the realm. Her adult life on earth was chaotic anguish.

She knows that her soul is now depleted of energy and needs to absorb all the love and vibrant fervour like a dry sponge soaking up a spill. Rest and loving healing given to her by each light being is already restoring her soul. She will process everything she's experiencing, and she will learn to surrender and lose her angst and replace it with peace, love, and forgiveness. This period with the light beings is only the beginning of a recuperation for her soul. All her senses will be revitalised. She'll take as long as she needs.

On earth, Asina is processing her own life and the life she shares with Nettie. The long journey has depleted her body. The separation for both women has been a release as well as a traumatic ending to life as they knew it on earth.

Nettie remains close with her mother and her children, and, as the days stretch into weeks since she left, each moment shared together opens yet another memory for Nettie and for the children. Each night, the children plop on their grandmother's bed, and they tell of their experiences with Nettie. How she laughed and cried, what made her laugh and cry. Nettie can feel their laughter and sadness, and she sits in the middle of them, coaxing them to keep talking out their feelings.

It's like any other night they gather, except, this time, they're surprised Nettie's buzzer sounds. The children haven't heard it before, and they sit spellbound and frightened. Asina reassures them it's just their mother as they all try to pull away to leave the room. The sound breaks up the group, but it also gives a sense of wonder and a feeling of protection to all.

Nettie is fully aware and joyful that her soul can now connect with her loved ones, especially her mother. Her purpose is to remain their guide, chaperon, mother, daughter, sister, aunt, niece, and friend. The bedside buzzer becomes a recognised communication between the two worlds. The children interpret the sound as a loving call from their mother. Asina considers the sound an urgent signal from Nettie, a warning message she needs to intuit.

She believes that Nettie is now warning Asina and the children to be ready for decisions to be made to her unfinished personal details she left behind. During her last months and weeks, Nettie was resistant to any impending encounter concerning any of her wishes.

Four days after the funeral, terror strikes through the children's hearts and into their souls. They run and strongly resist any attempt to remove them from the home they know was chosen by their mother for them. Nettie's message is validated. She encourages Asina to make the issue legal. Nettie insists her own voice is to be heard through her own testimony within her will. Her written words, "to remain in the care of the grandparents as guardians," loudly resound Nettie's sentiments, and she's insisting that her words will not be ignored.

So begins what becomes a long journey through the system for Asina and Sentel and the family. Nettie uses the buzzer for direction, advice, protection, or comfort each time a major decision or emotional trauma is experienced. Asina becomes accustomed to Nettie's input from the other side.

Daily, Asina struggles to comfort and console the children during their grief over the loss of their mother. Asina continues to hold long comforting sessions for whoever needs them on her bed each night. Most nights, all the children line the foot of her bed for comfort and soothing. The youngest usually crawls up and snuggles in beside Asina.

Their feelings encompass losing their mother and leader and their fear of being separated from each other. Their mother's intention of keeping them together was burnt into their psyche the day she expressed these wishes, her last wishes, to them before she could no longer verbally communicate. Asina knows that Nettie's last wishes will continue to manifest in the children—in their decisions and values throughout their future lives together.

Still, the issue of permanent residency persists in multiple hearings until the proceedings end as the children, torn and tattered, reach the age to choose for themselves. The siblings choose not to be separated. They continue to live with Asina and Sentel.

Asina finds that, through the years of battle, she hasn't allowed herself time to process her own grief. She finds herself struggling now with headaches, excessive tiredness, and nausea. She feels so overwhelmed and exhausted and doesn't know what to do with herself. She knows the build-up of post-traumatic stress disorder (PTSD) is taking its toll.

During her daytime chores, she finds she's feeling very unwell. The right side of her body is very heavy. She arrives home after another day at work and takes time to lay on the couch. She tries to settle, but the nausea begins and doesn't stop. Hours pass, and she's still retching. She tries to walk, but her right side fails her. Neena phones for an ambulance to take her to hospital. During the long trip to the city hospital, the paramedics medicate her to try to stop her heaving. Asina is desperate as the projectile vomiting increases.

After seven hours in the emergency department, treatment is exhausted, and Asina is still in and out of consciousness and still dry retching. She knows she has no control over the right side of her body, and she's frightened and aware of everything that's happening to her or being done by the doctors and nursing staff.

She believes she's having a stroke. She's at the same time very aware she's in the presence of Jesus. Spirits surround her, and she demands loudly, "Jesus, either heal me or take me home. Don't leave me living in this state. Please don't let me be a burden on the family by leaving me brain-damaged or unable to move my body. I'm of no use to anyone paralysed down one side of my body. Please don't take me from the children now. They've had enough sorrow. Please let me live to be of service to them, and let me be healed."

She regains consciousness. The doctor is standing near her, and a nurse is standing on the other side of her. Their faces tell her of their thoughts. Asina has stopped heaving so violently. They wheel her to another room for tests and then take her to a ward and get her into a bed. After hours of communicating with Jesus and the spirits, Asina is still alive, but exhausted. She settles in her bed and knows she's been answered and healed.

In the morning, her nurse tells her, "The nurse who was with you last night in emergency called in this morning to see if you'd made it through the night. She was amazed when I told her that you're alive, and there's no damage to your body. She sends you her best wishes for a full recovery."

Asina's equally amazed that she made it through. She's validated by the nurse's story and lies in her bed believing that she had a choice of leaving, and she chose to stay on earth and finish her assignment. She rolls over and holds her rosary beads close to her heart, believes, and whispers to herself, "God is good."

Lying in the hospital bed for the next few days, Asina knows how easy it would have been for her to leave her body behind and join Nettie on the other side. She longs for her child and wonders how she'll live her days without her. A deep sorrow encompasses her entire body, with a heaviness like lead in her arms and legs, and she realises this is the first time she's allowed herself to begin to heal the loss. Part of her really did want to go home. "Rest your body, Mum," she hears Nettie tell her. She closes her eyes and dozes off to sleep somewhere in between earth and heaven.

The children arrive at night and take over her bed with her in it. They laugh and giggle and poke fun at her, and at once she feels alive again. They ignite her soul. She responds to them with love and assurance and tells them that all is well. They bring little gifts of chocolates and sweets for her, and they sit and eat them for her.

When she's ready to go home, they arrive with their aunt, and Asina and her entourage, who are each carrying her belongings, march out of the hospital as one impressive force to be reckoned with.

Asina is to take time off work and recuperate her energy at home. Chores are shared, and Asina needs to soak up the sunshine in her dilapidated garden. She hasn't touched it for years, although Sentel has managed to weed it and save her potted plants by planting them out. He also created a new special garden for Nettie.

Asina wanders the large front garden and looks at the trees she'd planted from seedlings years ago. They reach high into the blue sky, telling Asina that it's been a long time since she noticed them. She realises that there are many things that have gone unnoticed since Nettie became sick.

Soon after Nettie left, Asina's beautiful black Labrador passed away, and it's only now that she really notices he's not there with her. Her tiny cat also passed shortly after the dog. She tears up when she thinks about them.

The new dog, bought for the youngest child, is a gem. It has sidled up to Asina, and, slowly, she's allowing herself to open to it. The children allow it on the couch and bring it onto Asina's bed at night for their visit. Asina recoils from getting close to it and doesn't want it in her domain. Of course, the children don't listen.

Winter arrives, and Asina beds the new dog down in its warm blankets and goes to her room to sleep. Somewhere in the middle of the night, the dog makes its way onto Asina's bed and snuggles up to her warmth. Asina wakes in the morning looking into its big black eyes, and she's too tired to yell at it, so she falls back to sleep. Now it's allowed on the end of her bed. Sometimes, Asina wants to cuddle the dog up to her so badly, yet she won't allow herself the experience. Maybe, one day, this battle inside will cease for Asina.

PART 7

Heaven

14

Life Review

WITHIN THE ENCLOSED SANCTUARY OF LIGHT and tenderness, Nettie's soul experiences a full review of every event encountered in the last lifetime. Her soul needs to align this new awareness into reality.

Choices and behaviour that have been lived through impact her soul. The process begins with the joyful memories of being born into a family of love and generosity as the youngest child. Her position as the last child in the family existed for a long time before two others joined in the line-up. The first four were born just three years apart, and memories of the closeness and acceptance within the group of siblings come flooding through to her soul.

Shortly after the arrival of Nettie's soul on earth, the family moved to an isolated island as sole residents. Here, they lived in silence, away from society and in hope and survival among the makeshift facilities the island threw at them. Nettie was only little when they arrived at their home, and she lived a small child's life on the small patch of land in the sheltered bay.

She realises she was angry with her parents for leaving her at night with her siblings, thinking she was asleep in the beachside tent they lived in for a year while the house was being renovated. Now, she sees her parents are only a short distance from the tent, huddling around the warm fire having toast and jam with hot billy tea.

A great forgiveness and gratitude surges through her. Through new eyes, she understands her concerned parents and sees the complicated cough that she developed from the fear of being left alone. Her parents started taking her out to the fire with them to alleviate the cough and her fear. She realises they knew her well.

All her many fears raise their heads. She fears going to the outside toilet, day and night, in case she falls in the deep hole in the ground of the makeshift thunderbox. She fears getting on the boat, as she might throw up all over her siblings, which she did many times. She fears the cattle calling to each other at night, the strange noises of the incoming tide that might reach her, the water lapping on the beach, and the night animals on the prowl.

Her young anxieties become a part of her adult life. They never did go away completely. They just changed from situation to situation throughout her life. She sees the impact on others. She's surprised and sad at the same time.

Formal education through homeschooling and incidental environmental education were part of her daily chores of existence. The group of four were their own playmates, and the close bond tightened between them. This bond exists through death and into the spiritual realm. Her soul looks back to the family's interactions during this time and can see the part she played as the family group reached out to children in need of the love of a family and invited them into their family.

Caring and stretching beyond personal wants and desires were integral parts of the life of the family, and these traits became embedded in her throughout the rest of her life. Her soul remembers there were squabbles amongst the family group, misunderstandings between her and the new arrivals, sibling rivalries, parental corrections of the young ones, parents bickering, and she especially experiences the hurtful effects she had on the others at that age. However, sharing and unconditional love were the significant lessons gained by the entire family during this time.

Memories progress now to when the family arrived back on the mainland and all the children were sent to a mainstream school for the first time. This experience was difficult for the children. They reached out to others to play with, but it wasn't so easy. They became aware of the school rules and procedures. Mingling socially became easier after a while, and new friendships flourished.

Life became regular again, but different. She'd brought her unconditional love and sharing with her, and she now realises that the lessons learned as a young child became part of her as a young adult. She could connect her decisions of reaching out to those in need to her decision to love someone who didn't know how to love and would deny love and sustenance to her and their children. Her soul both cringes at this realisation and sees and feels the love given but not returned. There is no failure.

She sets out to watch and experience the upheaval between the couple again. Hurtful words spoken by her, as well as words unspoken that turned into hurtful thoughts and actions. These thoughts emitted toxic energy into the couple and family environment. She experiences each one again and finally experiences it from the others' points of view. Her soul feels how her children took each comment as their own, and how they impacted their young lives. She witnesses how those times are still causing the children great anguish to this day as she watches from her spiritual abode.

Her soul experiences the desertion and betrayal again and the impact it had on her body, resulting in cancer and death. She feels the anger and rage stir in her and experiences the lack of understanding and awareness extended to her.

In turn, compassion wells up and truth resonates from within her soul's awareness as she feels the other's lack of being loved and nurtured as a child and experiences humility and honour for the soul. Her soul realises the extent of wisdom remaining to be gained—without anger and rage, but with compassion.

Her soul relives each birth of her children. The happiness mixed with the pain. The honour mixed with the overwhelming anxiety. The excitement mixed with fear. She feels each tiny little hand in hers, grasping for love and protection. She feels the lack of know-how, coupled with the responsibility placed in her hands. She feels the overpowering love surge through her as she welcomes each child into the world.

Uniting the children together in love becomes her purpose as a mother. Blending the love into the children requires spiritual assistance. Building a physical home for the family is paramount and is achieved through perseverance and hard work. The hardships of raising a family appear in the first few years. Couplehood takes a back seat as each child arrives and finds its place in the group. Cracks appear. Her soul feels and experiences all the arguments and silences. She feels the sickness in her belly developing.

She persists in reviewing these times. She battles for her family. She feels all the other's pains and misunderstandings. At this time on earth, she decides that she won't be able to watch as the progress through life entails receiving the consequences of choices made.

The children came to surround her with their love. She feels their intensity surging through her soul, willing her to live, regardless. She honours her children, and she now surrounds herself with their love. She remembers leaving a note to them in her last days, and she notices they have this note with them. They've framed it and hung it on their wall to remember her in their home. She expresses her sentiments to them in her last writings, in her own handwriting, written especially to them.

When the review closes and the wise ones' assistance is completed, their directions are offered to Nettie's soul. "You may choose to go back to a further life on earth or to remain here." She ponders her options and decides to gain further knowledge before returning to earth.

Synchronously, an immense energy rises within Asina. She, too, feels her life review while on earth. Her values change. No longer does she judge others nor dwell on her self-loathing thoughts. Through the consequence of Nettie's death, she's more accepting of Nettie's life. Although she misses Nettie, she tries to understand the decision Nettie has made to go home, and Asina no longer blames herself for failing her daughter.

Almighty power and strength are the spiritual results of Asina walking in the present moment, day to day, to reach the conclusion. Hope, loss, survival, and belief are the spiritual gifts given to Asina for her to walk into the full circle of life—with Nettie beside her as she continues to raise the children. No longer is she silent.

After Asina reviews her past with Nettie, she sits and ponders her own time of death. She says to herself, "Death will come quickly to me when my heart is tired. I will traverse the black void, and I, too, will call the name of my master, Jesus, telling Him that I'm home. The beautiful Goddess in the light will appear at the doorway. I will enter the room flooded with intense light with her. I will encounter the master of light, who will lead me to many luminaries deliberating around a huge table. I, too, will exist only in that moment."

Chronic turmoil has eased in the family, and now it's time to safely assess the damage caused by the devastating damage and loss.

For Asina, she likens the family's loss to a torrential rain that has deluged the countryside. Flooding waters have thundered down the mountain slopes into the valleys below. The creeks have broken their banks, and the people, their houses, their animals, and the soils of the plains have all been washed away into the torrents of water, gushing through the local creeks and rivers and out to the mouths of these rivers into the open sea.

For those who have survived, their farmlands are waterlogged, and the dwellings left standing are inundated with putrid, muddy water. Survivors are dazed and displaced. Fresh water for drinking is mixed with filth, food produce is lain bare on their fields, and belongings are mixed with the fallen crops.

As with the floods, Asina is faced with the impact of survival on the children, their displacement from their home and environment. Their unpacked belongings are stacked in boxes throughout Asina's sheds and offices. There is also their unsettled studies, their craving for what was, the gathering of remnants left scattered amidst the chaos and dust.

The impact on the rest of the family, and, when she gets around to it, on herself, is not easy for her. She's realising she can hold less and less to her unwavering stance since Nettie left. She has held on during these survival years without crying and without allowing the overwhelming feelings of loss wash her out to sea.

15

⟨Balance

EVERYONE IN THE FAMILY NEEDS TO be back facing their future lives and realising the drama is no more. Peace for their souls is becoming a part of their lives for the first time. Asina knows it will take some time for their minds and bodies to process the transformation. But the need for a new beginning has begun and will continue.

Creativity of study, work, and craft is opening the desires of weary souls. Nettie's activities of trips to the beach, concerts, sporting events, camping, parties, shopping trips, gardening, refurnishing their rooms, watching DVDs, eating ice cream, having sleepovers with cousins, building cubby houses, picnics on the lounge floor, visits to other family and friends, travelling, fishing, swimming, art, cooking, cleaning, air flights, playing, playing, and more playing are all revived by the children and taken on by the adults in the family.

Asina knows she hasn't opened to her soul, and that she's the only one left to be attended to. She's aware of the processes of grief, but cannot seem to open her own feelings. She knows she's holding back her intense emotions.

She sits sometimes on her own and allows her reactions to rise, but she cannot cry. As quickly as they appear, they disappear even quicker. "What will it take to open my soul, dear Mary?" she asks each night of her Goddess. She tries to meditate, to pray, to talk to the Holy Spirit, but she can no longer interact fully.

Then, Neena is unexpectedly hurt. This event sends ripples of shock and terror through Asina's mind and body. It's as if an arrow has been shot through her heart. She doubles up in pain. She cries. No one understands her intensity. She tries to block up her emotions. She manages to block her hurt, but her anger is not blocked. The family don't understand what's happening to their rock. No one can soothe her. No circumstances can convince her body to settle.

For weeks, Asina is unreachable. She's feeling the deluge of flooding rains all over again. She's spiralling into a depression quickly. All are concerned. She knows she's completely in a hyper-aroused state. She tells the family, "I've climbed up a tree like a cat being chased by a dog, and I've gone too far out on a limb. I can't get down."

Asina is concerned. It has been a long, long time since she's allowed herself to endure such an out-of-control internal commotion. Even when Nettie passed over to the other side, she'd had no reactions like the present withdrawal. Or had she? Or has she been in a withdrawn state since Nettie first became sick?

Asina remembers that she ended up in hospital when Nettie was first diagnosed. She managed to shut off the waste disposal system in her body for weeks. Withdrawal from her bodily and mental functioning were all part of massive stress on an already weakened body.

Now she disintegrates into a withdrawn confusion. She is slipping quickly into an unresponsive state. Her body is breaking out in tremors, and her mind blanks out at any minute. She becomes afraid of driving, working, shopping, or going out anywhere on her own. The family take over her mundane jobs and daily chores.

She finally calls for help from her family. She sits one night and explains clearly what she's feeling. The threat of having another of her children hurt and in danger of dying is just too much for her to comprehend. She explains how her mind and body adjust to threats by withdrawing from the threat and creating a silent haven behind closed ears, eyes, thoughts, and bodily functions. Asina has travelled into severe survival mode without being aware of her actions.

She gains understanding that she's been in this prolonged state of survival for too long. She's been functioning like this before and since Nettie's death with a multitude of chores to do, including tending to Nettie, arranging her funeral, attending to legal issues, soothing children, losing pets, running the business, putting together others' lives, and keeping her true emotions far away from her consciousness.

Neena's needs shattered Asina's already deteriorated body, one that has protected her soul throughout the years of grieving the sickness of her child through to her death and to her own acceptance of her loss. Asina corrects herself, thinking, *No one gets away with not facing buried emotions. It's time for me to grieve. To grieve the loss of Ralia, Ezara, Lucah, Gus, Siroda, and Nettie.*

Accumulated grief is rattling at the very core of Asina's soul. No longer can she be the staunch warrior who charges into battle with a guttural war cry that can be heard and answered in the spirit world where she belongs. It's from the spirit world that she receives her strength to continue the battle to survive her seven steps to heaven.

She has reached her core, the soul she arrived with from heaven. She has endured becoming her soul while on earth.

She can cry and won't be belted for it. She can grieve and won't lose control. She can speak with no fear of reprisal when there is injustice. She can open her soul to all the wonders of the love she has infused in the many children she has cared for.

She can let Ralia go in peace without feeling the horror of her leaving. She can own the love of her sister, Ralia. Over the years, Ralia has shared visits with Asina, and both shared their children with each other when they were young. Ralia pulled away from Asina when she lost her child. Asina is aware that Ralia knows what that loss is like, and she also knows what the loss of a family is like. In her later years, she and Asina fell distant. Asina has allowed spirit to organise another meeting of the sisters.

Asina grieves Ezara all over again. She experiences her mother come to her in spirit and encourages Asina to remain in her soul. Ezara shows herself to Asina through signs of special times spent together, like Christmas. Asina feels the excitement of Christmas with Ezara when she sends visions of a beautiful, large, shining star, sparkling in the dark sky. There's a huge Christmas tree glowing with coloured lights and adorned with tinsel and decorations and presents opened each Christmas with her mother. A child's excitement now fills Asina when the vision sets itself indelibly into her soul. Asina will never forget her mother again. She is so grateful to her mother.

Lucah floods her memory. She remembers seeing the girl she loved years after his death, at a ceremony in the city. Engrossed in the talk given on thankfulness for those who loved and cared for you in your greatest times of need, both find each other in the crowd, and their eyes meet. A moment set by spirit and Lucah to have both souls making peace with each other in the surrounds of peace and harmony.

Forgiveness and pain transformed into love in that moment that was set, with Lucah and spirit as guides in love. This is the moment with Lucah in spirit that Asina will never forget.

Gus decided to leave earth just months prior the terror of 9/11. In Asina's mind, Gus wouldn't have believed such a thing was possible. Asina had been to visit him on and off through to his eventual demise in the nursing home. He had been a provider in the home, but he'd never really been an endearing character his children could get close to. He'd believed in corporal punishment, and he'd used it especially on Asina. She'd become his scapegoat for all his rage.

One year, when the anniversary of the twin towers was nearing, Asina was perturbed by the fact that many under the rubble were never found. She obsessed on this truth and pleaded to spirit to help her process the grief. Soon after, Gus came to her in spirit in a dream. Asina found herself under the monument where many were at rest, and he came to her there and reassured her not to worry, as they were all safe and at home in spirit. Asina never again felt the pangs of death surrounding the anniversaries of 9/11, nor felt that her father was disinterested in her. She was pleased he had comforted her and believes that he is one of her guides from the spirit world.

Siroda lived on for nearly ten years after Gus left. She mellowed from her bitter self after Asina took her home with her for some time, until she finally went to a home for the aged near her. Even though she was not sick, nor suffered dementia, Siroda knew that Asina could not look after her without outside help. Before she left earth, Siroda admitted to Asina that she should have never left her with Ezara. She made no excuses or apologies to Asina for her decision.

Asina was pleased Siroda told her this, as it validated that Siroda felt the pain of her decision. It became a sense of healing for Asina. Siroda also came with spirit after she passed. She came wearing a beautiful white dress with deep blue trims. Asina remembered the beautiful dresses Ezara would make for her daughter. In that moment, the three women became one together. A deep healing took place for each of them. The truth is the truth, and death didn't take the truth away. Asina has two mothers who love her in spirit in their own way, as she loves them.

16

Harmony

ASINA KNOWS NETTIE IS ALWAYS WITH her. She feels Nettie's spirit present in the most minute ways that keep her aware. A butterfly landing on her collar as she walks the dog. A little blue wren sitting in the tree outside her window. Something that is lost is found with an ask to Nettie.

She questions Nettie in how she wants the children raised. What she wants to give them for birthdays and Christmas. What courses they need to take in high school or university. Every day, Nettie is talked about freely by the children and the family.

Asina refuses to withdraw from Nettie as she did with Ezara, although she struggles each day since Nettie's death not to succumb to her old habit of disconnecting. The battle to remain open is excruciating for Asina, as it's easier for her to detach for the needs of the children and for the endless chores of creating a new life that are always occupying her mind. Even though she knows her suffering is unbearable without her daughter around her constantly, she still will protect her soul and resist touching her deepest spirit.

PTSD raises itself regularly in Asina's psyche. She is conscious of the need to care physically for her mind and body, but has only sparingly committed to achieving results over the last years.

Through Neena's incident, Asina has become fully aware of her deep reactions and understands not to withdraw from her soul either. She allows her present, continuing, thunderous emotions, aggravated by Neena's pain, to pass through her heart to her soul. Creating harmony with her soul through acceptance of her choice of this lifetime has become her blessing. She is her soul.

Nettie's own choices led her with Asina on a different spiritual path. One of exploration of life and death. Of becoming soul together.

Harmony between heaven and earth is obvious to Asina as she walks both sides each day. Her childhood and her adulthood have become one existence, stretching from her arrival on earth to her pending departure. There is no demarcation line between the two realms. There is only the warmth of love, encompassing the whole.

"I get it," Asina says. "I get it now!"

She rests her weary eyes and says to the spirit realm, "Show me as I go to sleep what I need for tomorrow."

Asina feels an answer to her prayers upon awakening next morning and feels the spirit inspire her to get up out of her PTSD thoughts and plan a three-hour trip to the beach for a break with Sentel. She reminds herself, *It has been so long since we sat on the beach together.* She recognises, *We need to review our relationship as a couple after fifty-two years.*

Asina rises early for her birthday. She feels complete. There is only wonder in her. Wonder and honour for earth's beauty and heaven's accessibility. Never has she seen this dimension so clearly. Today, it gives her a great sense of inner peace and harmony within the universe.

She is met with warm scones and fruit and a cup of tea from her grandchildren. They ignite her passion for art with a gift of canvases and paints. Her soul is craving an expression, now that it's open. She feels distant from her past. She has Ezara, Nettie, and Lucah in her present and future. There is no longer the need to look behind. All is happening in the present moment. The day progresses with more family to celebrate her day. By nightfall, Asina accepts her grief has thawed and melted into rivers of life-giving water flowing from heaven to enrich her life.

With these thoughts in mind, Asina and Sentel pack their new car. This is the first weekend they can get away after owning the car for twelve months. Their intention in buying the fastest car was to have the fastest retirement once every couple of months, on their own.

They had to work the morning and lunch shifts and resolve a few family issues before leaving, so they set out on the three-hour journey later in the afternoon, hoping they would make it to the resort before nightfall.

They take a shortcut off the highway, onto a bumpy and winding mountain road that stretches their anxieties a little, but they know it's quicker. Somehow, they both silently think they really are going to beat the foreboding darkness.

Asina sees a sign warning motorists to be aware of wildlife using the road. Another anxiety is added to the already long list. She thinks Sentel, too, has perhaps seen the sign. *Thank God he didn't panic me*, she thinks to herself, knowing full well that kangaroos eat at this time of day, and they could cause severe damage, if not kill them, if they jumped in front of their car.

They reach the highway in the dark. That anxiety is now released, and driving in the dark becomes the next anxiety. They take their exit and follow the road to the resort. Yes, they're going to be okay. They take all the correct turns, but they don't make it.

They're left trying another road from the southern approach. No, they don't make it. Now their anxieties are really being felt. Sentel is about to have a meltdown.

Asina heads for the northern approach to the township. Sentel gives up at this point. "We're right now," she convinces him. Coming from this approach seems to be going well for them, and anxieties ease, until Asina finds she's back to the place where she was before. She phones the resort.

"Oh, you're just five minutes away," the receptionist replies. "Go back to the last set of traffic lights, turn right, and turn right at the end of that road and follow the next road until you see us on your left. We are lit up like a Christmas tree. You can't miss us." They see the lights ahead. Asina says to Sentel, "They are lit up like a Christmas tree." They don't miss it this time.

Sentel sighs deeply as he arrives at the resort. "Ahh! Only took us six hours to do a three-hour trip!"

Asina replies, "It shows we can harmonise well together." They both muster up a laugh.

They settle in for a few days of rest. They know they need it. They are frazzled from work, family commitments, and the years of turmoil. They just sleep, eat, and walk on the beach for the first day.

The next day, Asina silently reflects on her many years with Sentel as her companion. She sees him standing beside her through Ezara's and Lucah's leaving. She sees him grieving with her for Nettie and silently fighting with her through the legal battles. She sees him willingly take responsibility for the welfare of his family by still rising each day to go to work to keep them safe and secure. She knows his love for Nettie exceeds his fears of not following normal social expectations for his age, like retiring. She also knows his greatest challenge has been combatting his negativity to keep going forward each day. Asina accepts in her soul that he has fulfilled his life's mission to warn, protect, and keep her safe through all their unconventional activities of seeking justice for the broken children who found their way to the couple.

On the last day of their stay, spirit speaks clearly to Asina as she prays for guidance, as they both still feel they are not coping as well as they have been able to in the past. Spirit answers the couple by allowing them to see that, when they cared for many children throughout their years together, it was all in preparation for this time in their lives.

Asina shares her feelings with Sentel. "Together, we cared for and loved all the children we were sent, and each had their own story. We did our best to help them resolve their issues, but the issues overflowed into our problems. Looking back now, we can see that their problems were not ours personally."

Asina continues, "As parents it is hard to disentangle your children's issues from your own personal issues. There's a difference in carrying your children's issues to just being their guiding lights and not letting their lives absorb your own lives!"

They both ponder these thoughts as they walk hand in hand along the beach. Asina reaches a solution. "We can now detach from their pain and sorrow and see ourselves as merely instruments God uses us to love them. We can see we're okay. We don't have the problems. We just walk together with them."

That day, they know God has them safely in His hands. Sentel seeks Asina's confirmation as he asks her, "Then there is no need to fear the past thoughts of something wrong with our relationship?"

Asina hugs him and reaffirms, "There's nothing wrong with us, Sentel."

Many times, they have been brought to the understanding that, without their completeness, each of their souls' purpose on earth would not come to fruition. Their couple relationship challenges them still today, as they are opposites working together to create a completeness. But they do harmonise well.

They both know the time will come when one of them will leave for home first. On their last night at the resort, they look into each other's eyes, into each other's souls, and find a sense of acceptance and peace. They light-heartedly ponder together the scenario where they will both leave earth together. Sentel insists, "That's the only possible way." They both agree.

In a quieter moment, each of them feels the sensation of being separated from each other and the loneliness that will follow. Sentel knows that Asina is waiting to see heaven. He is not so sure about leaving just yet.

Of course, the grandchildren have other ideas and tell their grandparents constantly, "You are to live past a hundred! Both of you!"

Asina hears a call from the children. "Grandma, where are you? Grandma!"

Home again, Asina stirs from her comfortable position of sitting in her armchair in the afternoon sun, and she straightens her sun hat and as she stands. She feels the warmth of healing spreading throughout her body. "Oh, I feel better," she muses. "My anxiety has passed. The battle inside me seems to have eased," she tells herself. "I no longer feel the need to run from my feelings. Or to run to tend to the children as I have done since Nettie left."

Asina moves forward with a little skip in her stride. She can be assured that the children are safe with her now. She knows all they want from her is to come and start another meal for everyone and to feed the noisy dog.

As the sun goes down on another day, Sentel takes the youngest child and goes to hand-feed the cows and to check their water. It has been nearly nine years since the last heavy drenching of rain soaked their land, and the drought still doesn't look like it's lifting over their country area. He buys cattle fodder regularly and uses the house bore to water them, as the farm wells are dry and cannot water them nor water the vegetation. He also needs to order more drinking water for the family. They manage to use a tankful in three to four weeks. Asina takes the clothes in from the line before they get blown away with the winter westerlies that blow dust through cracks and crevices in windows and doors of the house.

The two older children meet her in the kitchen to help clear the mess from their afternoon snacks, wash their dishes, and gather vegetables to be prepared for the meal. Asina can now begin their evening meal.

Once it's dark, and after the outside chores are completed, everyone is inside. In the kitchen, with pots and pans bubbling and spitting, fresh food aromas beckon appetites to be ready for a feast. Everyone's chatter of the day's events fills the room and this homely atmosphere. The room is swarming with love, companionship, story sharing, giving to and receiving from each other, all coupled with the latest music playing from the CD player.

For Sentel and Asina, it's a young home once again. Grandparents move to become young parents again and accompany the children to pop concerts and young cinema shows. They attend school events and line up for parent interviews.

Grandchildren sip hot tea from cups with saucers and read the newspapers with their grandfather and search for upcoming entertainment events to which they can take their grandparents. They experience the work ethic of older people by working with Asina and Sentel, who still run the same store after all these years. They learn to work with staff, and the older ones can now manage the store while Sentel and Asina retire for their few days every other month.

Happiness reigns once again for the family, who have created a unified whole. The group continues to meld into their new creation of what a family means to them.

After the meal, Asina rests in her armchair with her cup of tea. She casts her mind back to the happiness she felt when she found Ezara again, through Nettie's unintended wanderings into her past. She remembers the time she and Nettie were bonding together and made the promise to each other that they would find the "how" to exist this time. She remembers Nettie's words while lovingly holding hands with her—*We will set out to do the impossible, whatever that is, at all costs, and no matter what happens, we will support each other with the intention that we will find another way to exist.*

Asina sets out to evaluate in her mind the outcome of their promises made long ago.

She realises she has come to believe that, together, she and Nettie are continuing to create a new existence together on earth, encapsulated in the freedom the family is living each day. She also believes Nettie's consciousness continues in a new existence in the heavenly realm, within the freedom of her soul.

She stops and reflects with Nettie. *Never did we imagine back then, when we were together on earth, that we would find us sharing love and life together between the two realms as another way to exist.* She smiles and feels the humour come through from Nettie, reacting to Asina's statement.

She continues reflecting with Nettie. *We were also unable to imagine how our promises to each other were to play out across the two realms.*

Nettie's words once again reverberate in Asina's soul. *With the love that resides deep within us for each other, we will remain present and aware as a state of being, for each other and for ourselves.*

She solemnly realises their love for each other does remain with their intention to heal themselves and the family. They achieved the impossible at all costs, as well as healed the souls of the women who guided them from heaven.

Asina recognizes that the conversation is now becoming a three-way interaction as Asina contemplates a message she's receiving from spirit as she sits on her own.

Spirit explains, *The cost of freedom for the good of all is a soul's perfect intention.*

Asina is astounded with the statement and ponders the magnitude of the meaning.

She looks at the road she and Nettie continue to travel across the realms and recalls their further intentions. *No one will get left behind, and we will walk with each other to the end of the journey.*

"Ah! Nettie my love," Asina calls to her daughter. "I believe we live our answers to our questions. We found the "how" by changing our thoughts and beliefs to become present to our souls on earth. We answered the "why." We suffer to feel the deep emotions of love and survival on earth, to open our souls. Through answering the questions, we have become our souls to reach heaven. No one gets left behind, as our journey doesn't end with death. Our journey continues together for eternity."

Asina accepts that the cost of freedom for the good of all really is a soul's perfect intention. Asina is at peace with the outcome.

Peacefully, she remembers Ezara's little black purse that lies in her own kitchen cabinet. Her mind wanders back throughout the years as its keeper, and she remembers how many times she vulnerably held the purse to her heart.

She knows in becoming her soul through the earthly steps of her suffering and loss, she's now braver in speaking up for others who cannot. She's stronger in standing for what is right and just. She can now easily show compassion and love to herself as well as to humanity.

She understands only courage and honesty ooze from the little black purse, and Ezara's leading her on to continue to share their stories she came to tell.

Asina takes another sip of tea and stares out the window into the darkness of the night. She ponders the thought, *Who will be the next keeper of these teachings that have been gathered through the five generations? Who will be the next keeper of the little black purse?*

Asina closes her eyes and whispers to God, "Your will be done."

EPILOGUE

In this era where extensive technology exists in our lives, the element of surprise at the many natural wonders still thrives among us as we travel the globe as tourists and students of the world. The world is open for all to discover the natural causes of major happenings like tsunamis, earthquakes, volcanoes, weather, space, the universe, and the rise of humanity.

As we proceed into the future, we must not lose sight of the advances our ancestors forged out to bring us to the present time. Many lives were lost fighting for freedom. Many lives have been spared to live this era.

When we live long enough, we begin to see the human cyclic pattern of the seven steps of silence, hope, suffering, loss, believe, and becoming soul again in heaven repeating itself throughout the centuries. When we are aware of this pattern, we realise that we have the power to transform the next cycle into becoming our souls.

Modalities such as alternative medicines, health and well-being courses, and techniques such as mindfulness, are being presented constantly along with ever-new healing therapies. These therapies created in disciplines such as medicine, psychology, science and spirituality are to enhance our choices of how to live and how to heal our bodies, minds, and souls.

The simple story of Jesus and his family and friends, a story that happened over two thousand years ago, still resembles each of our own stories today. There are many therapies, techniques, and strategies that have been created since Jesus's time, ones that have never been thrown out or discarded, and ones that needed throwing out and discarding.

But the question always remains for each of us to answer.

Why do we have to experience the seven steps of silence, hope, suffering, loss, and survival to be able to believe, and to be able to become our soul again in heaven?

The introduction of this book suggests that we all leave home with the message: Your memory of who you are will fade. You will not remember what tasks you have set. It's your goal to search in each of your experiences while on earth for the lessons to be gained. Luminaries will meet you in many forms throughout this new lifetime. It will depend on you to recognise them and accept or decline their servitude.

This message suggests that luminaries will lead us to healing modalities, for they are aware we will meet each of our seven steps. We come in silence; we have young hopes for the future; we suffer through life; we lose loved ones through death; we either survive life and find our soul, or we choose not to survive. We either live without our soul's awareness on earth or leave this life and go home to realise we are soul once again.

To survive on earth, it's suggested we can choose to accept the guidance of heavenly luminaries or accept guidance through spiritual healers working on the earth. We can choose to believe we are soul or choose to believe we are not.

Jesus passes through His seven steps during His life on earth, and His life teaches us to follow our own seven steps as the way back to our soul.

He tells us there will be times of silence when no one will listen to us.

Have you been silenced? Have you experienced when no one will believe you? Have you had times when no one understands you? Have you spoken, but you are not heard?

He shows us that there will be times of hope for us when joy will fill us, and we'll see a brighter future.

Do we have hope and joy when our children are born? When they excel in their achievements? When they honour us as parents and carry on the love and peace they learnt through us?

He shows us there will be times of suffering in our lives.

We know these times come to us when a loved one suffers from illness or we suffer through illness, or when we suffer a brutal relationship, a betrayal by a loved one or friend, or we suffer our country at war.

Suffering turns to loss, as shown in the life of Jesus.

How many times have we lost friends or family through misunderstandings, betrayal, or the death of a beloved?

Survival is a built-in mechanism. It's our instinct. It's fight or flight. Times of chronic survival can take lives or cause disease. They can also strengthen the will to live or weaken our resolve to live.

Through strengthening the will, we learn to believe in our own power as an individual, our own power of choice, and we can use our power of awareness to become our soul.

Jesus survived all these emotions without turning to anger, hatred, and revenge. He didn't defend His case when brought to trial. By showing us how to live, He answers why we live through our earthly lives with trials and misfortunes. He leads us to the way home through our own seven steps. With His love, He supports us in becoming soul.

In the story, Asina walks her seven steps and finds her soul through the silent life of a child by loving and receiving love through Ezara. As an adult, she finds hope through loving and caring for others, and she learns suffering and loss through the death of her loved ones.

During the prolonged illness and unbearable death of her own child, she's broken open to her core by suffering. She is full of raw emotions, and her body reacts severely to the enormous stress inflicted on her. She is weakened physically, mentally, and spiritually, but chooses to survive the battle of becoming her soul.

She chooses to stay on earth and guide her grandchildren to their souls. In doing so, she strengthens her resolve to survive the death of her daughter, although the loss is great, and her aging body just wants to give up.

Nettie, her daughter, lives her seven steps throughout her lifetime on earth. She becomes her soul through her illness. She comes to understand she's more than her ravaged body. She believes she's her soul and returns to heaven. By releasing her soul to heaven, she gives her children the freedom to choose a future unencumbered by family hostility, and she teaches them why to choose to become their own souls at all costs.

The tale of the two women becoming their souls by living through the seven steps is only one story. It's hoped that their story will ignite the reader's own story, and, through their connection with spirit, the reader will be able to find their way back home, understanding and accepting why we all walk the seven steps to reach our souls.

Once we are aware that we are soul, we may choose to go home, or we may choose to stay to assist other souls to understand who they are and guide them through their own seven steps so they, too, will once again become their soul.

The intention is to weave throughout the story of Asina and Nettie the graces that they are granted from being in contact with spirit and with souls in heaven and the ability to translate these important messages into earthly meanings.

The story is not too far from the reality for many people who have struggled to find their own souls amidst the turmoil of daily life. This book is written to encourage the reader to continue on their own journey of soul-searching, and if they have already found their inner strength and their soul, the book is to express love and support to them as they continue to travel their journey of becoming soul to reach heaven.

May God bless each reader, and may He send His spirit of love to them and their loved ones.